Dirty Work

Also by Gabriel Weston

Direct Red

Dirty Work

A Novel

Gabriel Weston

LITTLE, BROWN AND COMPANY

NEW YORK BOSTON LONDON

Little, Brown and Company
Hachette Book Group
237 Park Avenue, New York, NY 10017
littlebrown.com

First North American Edition, August 2014
Originally published in Great Britain by Jonathan Cape, June 2013

Little, Brown and Company is a division of Hachette Book Group, Inc. The Little, Brown name and logo are trademarks of Hachette Book Group, Inc.

The publisher is not responsible for websites (or their content) that are not owned by the publisher.

The Hachette Speakers Bureau provides a wide range of authors for speaking events. To find out more, go to hachettespeakersbureau.com or call (866) 376-6591.

ISBN 978-0-316-23562-4
LCCN 2014934755

10 9 8 7 6 5 4 3 2 1

RRD-C

Printed in the United States of America

To my mother and father

Dirty Work

I have never seen so much blood.

My eyes can't take in the redness to start with. It's as if what I am looking at is the character of red, not the color, like looking at the sun, or staring into a fire. I try to blot the blood away, but as soon as I do this more comes, like a stream now. I reach for swabs, folding each one tightly in turn. Grasping them in my forceps I push them in, one after another, rotating my arm and wrist briskly as I do so. But my action only seems to make things worse.

How long this carries on, I do not know. Many minutes, perhaps half an hour. As long as it takes a person to die? This is what I am thinking at the moment when I feel the very walls shake. I wonder if there is an earthquake, whether the building is falling down, whether what is happening in my operating theater is, in fact, part of a wider, larger natural disaster, some outside catastrophe. Both doors fly open, and Frederick crosses the room in two strides. With hands under my arms, he lifts me off the operating stool and passes me over, like the pointless cargo I am. He sits down and holds out his wonderful large, veined hands for gloves, raising them up, palms open, fingers bent, as if in supplication. And once sheathed, these hands of his stay still for just a second or two, poised in the air before he picks up suction in one hand, forceps in the other. Before they descend into the pool of blood all around him, into the bleeding insides of my woman patient, just long enough to ask the anesthesiologist one question.

"Is she still alive?"

WEEK ONE

A good doctor needs to know how to spin a yarn. That's what they teach you at medical school, though no one ever says it in so many words. They prefer to give it a safe sort of name, the powers that be. They call it history-taking, this supposedly neutral process in which a patient and doctor collaborate to weave a shape out of what's gone wrong. They make it sound straightforward. And to the patient it probably feels that way. In reality, though, the competent clinical inquisitor is all the while asserting their own semantic frame, encouraging the patient to dwell on key symptoms, ignoring the white noise of emotion, veering away from anything that has no pathological meaning, doing what is necessary to help a diagnosis emerge. The doctor is rewriting the patient's story while seeming only to bear witness to it.

The second part of the doctor's quest, the clinical examination, is even more undemocratic. Here, all pretense of equality is done away with and the medic's interpretation takes over completely. Unless the voice or psyche is being examined, the patient must remain silent now, allowing the doctor to feel and listen to their body, to what it can tell them to counter or concur with the verbal details they have heard. The patient may not know it, but the body is in the dock, testifying for or against the character it houses.

I've tried to fly in the face of all this, to protect the sanctity of the patient's version of events, to eschew the medical convention which demands that a history should have a clear structure, a smooth finish and no loose ends. And look where it's got me. To this grim waiting room. To this leather chair where I sit, great with information, waiting to be ushered through that unopened door. To absolutely the wrong side of the investigative line, where it is now I who must submit to questions and a thorough grilling. And it turns out that all the hundreds of histories I have taken over the years have not prepared me one iota for the dreadful prospect of having my own reality doctored. I think this is the reason why we surgeons and physicians make the worst patients. It's not that we're more afraid of illness than the rest of you. It's because we're all hermeneutic tyrants, jealous guards of our own truths. Especially those we have kept quiet about.

My aunt owned a hotel when I was growing up, and we often visited my cousins there. When we did, as long as we didn't bother her with our prattle, we were free to roam over the whole establishment as if it were our home. My sister was still a baby, but my cousins and I loved to rampage around the place. We played noisy hide-and-seek under beds with fringed coverlets, and shouted in the dark-brown dining room when it was empty. We rushed to the clanking kitchen for snacks, and even went to the bar, as long as no guests were there.

It was underneath that bar that my boisterous play came to an end, though, and I learned real silence. I have no mental picture of the barman's face but I do remember the height of the barstools, and the way my cousins and I climbed up onto them, to the footrest first, and then the seat. This was always a bit precarious. Each stool was heavy as a cliff, and listed into the deep foresty pile of the carpet. You had to knee your way up and sit down really fast or it might tumble towards you, keel you over, push you to the ground.

I don't remember the barman's hands. But I do recall what these hands passed to me and my cousins as we sat on our stools, what lucky children we were as we sat there all three in a row, or sometimes two or even just one of us. The other two might be running down corridors connected by weighty doors with crisscross glass in their huge panes; or they might be outside in the bleached-grass garden in summertime, among the glare of flowers. It might just be one of us who chose to stay inside that cool, dark bar on an empty day with no one about.

I don't remember the smell of the corridors or of the garden, but I can recollect the whiff of the sweet cherries the barman put in my drinks, which he passed me with slow ceremony across the bar. They were in proper pretty cocktail glasses, and he filled them soundlessly with sticky juice. Each drink was given his very special attention and had a sharp stick in it, piercing a luminous maraschino cherry. The cherry against the juice was so bright it caused the body a tiny shock.

I find that my mind can't take me to the cellar without first going to the cherries. The cherries and the smell of them are the gateway through which my thoughts must pass before the next image comes, and I know I have reached this second scene when the olfactory memory of cherries changes sharply to one of urine.

I don't remember the barman's face. Instead, I think of dark words and see the dank floor. In my right hand, I am holding a bouncy rubber ball. It is marbled, a mixture of dark red and dark blue, and it fills my hand because my hand is small. I have been given this ball by the barman and I am bouncing it carefully on the concrete floor. It is that clever, hard kind of rubber that makes no noise. I am mindful to keep my eyes on the ground to make sure that the piece of concrete I drop it on is smooth enough to send the ball back into my palm, for it not to bounce off elsewhere, crazy-style, away from all the corners of this space. Or maybe this is not the reason I am looking at the floor.

Here I see myself from the outside as if I don't belong to myself anymore. The small and cobwebby window gives just enough light to show the barman and a young child standing among the brutish silhouettes of beer kegs. And what I see, as if from above, is a harsh fountain of very yellow pee arcing from its source to the concrete floor and splashing there, the little drops spraying up and wetting the girl's socks which are those white crochet ones, in blue Clarks sandals.

The last image I have is of the girl, one of her hands

holding a rubber ball and the other one holding the liverish penis of the barman. That is, insofar as her hand can reach around it. They are both standing in the puddle of urine, now at rest on the concrete floor. And all the things that were moving in this scene, the ball, the pee, the man, the child, are now so quiet and still.

The door opens on a young woman in brown. I am on my feet. I feel the heat of adrenaline in my limbs. But I have to sit down again. She tells me the panel of judges will only keep me waiting five more minutes then, without pausing for a response, she goes back into the meeting room.

Surely, you might ask, medical evidence comes to the rescue? Doesn't it tell the objective truth? However warped a patient's story may be by the way a doctor reconstructs it, there can't possibly be room for error in this empirical zone? But still I say that there is bias. Take biopsies, for example. Any pathologist, looking at a piece of tissue under a microscope, will tell you that their ability to reach an accurate diagnosis depends on the quality of the sample they are sent by their surgical colleagues.

An unhelpful sample may be too small, or messily excised. It might be taken from the wrong part of the lesion, or from the right place but confusingly orientated for the histologist's microscope. Sometimes, it has simply been badly preserved or labeled. Even in an expert's hands, such a biopsy is only capable of rendering a partial truth.

A good biopsy, on the other hand, is cut from a representative area of presumed disease. It is removed with sharp and generous margins. It is preserved and presented clearly in a way that elucidates how the excised area fits into the rest, so that this pathology may then be analyzed within the context of the body overall. There are more bad biopsies taken than good.

What, then, should I hand over for the pathologist's scrutiny? How will I select the right fragment to give to my judges?

When I went to tell my parents what had happened that day, words failed me. In fact, until we moved abroad a few years afterwards, it seemed as if I had lost my voice, somewhere in that dark cellar. For ages my mother allowed me to hide in the shadow of her, or among her skirts. If someone asked my name, she spoke for me. She let me hide myself away in the soft places of the house, nearest to wherever she might be: under the beds, in the airing cupboard, behind the sofas. I read in these safe corners and, at night, I was read to by my father, hearing his stories from a position of exquisite bedtime snugness, thrilled by the sense of security a duvet and my dad's proximity could give. But there was also the unforgiving empty shade of school, the place where, for all my attempts to remain inconspicuous, I was expected to shape up, to become a person for the world.

Even from the outside, my primary school looked gloomy, a Victorian building set in the middle of black asphalt. The playground roared with boys, and they invaded everywhere, including the outside loos, which I tried to hide in during break-time. These loos stank and had see-through crackly paper into which the pee didn't blot but ran off along its sharp creases into your hands.

The school was dark inside too, and huge, and full of an indistinct din. The classrooms had high ceilings, and old-fashioned desks with the chairs attached, and inkwells, and scored wooden lids that could snap down on your fingers at any time. The names of the teachers are a blank to me now, though I can call to mind the fat blond face of one of them who grabbed me by the nylon V-neck jumper one afternoon and said something mean to me because I had been asking her for a new reading book.

The door opens a second time. I think I might be sick. The woman in brown asks me in. Is my patient dead? Have I killed her? What about all the people I have tried to help? Do they no longer count? I follow the young woman through the doorway. I watch her suit. Will I ever wear my white coat again?

I enter my judgment chamber. My limbs, at least, still function as they should. I approach and sit in the chair meant for me. It is in the center of the room and faces a long conference table at which my opponents will sit. In some respects, it is like any of the other hospital seminar rooms in which I have listened to lectures or participated in tutorials over the years. But there are small differences. My judges' table is covered with a heavy green cloth. In the middle of the table there is an object. It has the shiny, heavy look of a trophy. I see the initials GMC emblazoned on its gleaming surface. There are other things on the table too, forms and pads of paper, a tray with a jug of water and a stack of Duralex glasses. It's the nearest I've ever got to stepping into a court of law. I wonder if I'll be asked to swear on the Bible before I speak.

I notice that the young woman with the brown skirt is at one end of the table, consulting papers. The room flutters with them, the light changes with her riffling. It is these details I must endeavor to pull myself away from. I feel my physical mass on the chair and the presence too of the other person in the room, just a little older than me, his blond hair as soft as a baby's, plaid sleeves rolled up over smooth forearms. He tries a smile but doesn't wait to see if he'll get one back. Perhaps he doesn't want me to witness the look on his face as he joins me up with my crime: not just this misdemeanor, but all the others he probably connects with it. He is a mouse of a man.

The room is perfectly square and family-planning-clinic beige. The carpet is thick. I hear the puff of the door opening and then "Good morning" behind me, in a woman's voice which would usually ring out, a voice used to making a brisk impact, although the acoustics of this room put a dampener on it. As she comes past my right side I see tiny holes in the pile where her suede aubergine heels wound the carpet. She carries a leather binder under one arm, bearing the same insignia as the metal statue on the table. A column of sun comes through the single window behind my judges' table and the room makes merry with her lipstick; all its corners receive her scent. She passes me in her pale suit and tips her femininity across the table as she shakes her colleagues' hands. Her fatness does not matter one bit. On the ward, we would call it centripetal obesity or lemon-on-a-stick. When she goes around the bank of chairs to take up the middle one, there mixes up in me, with her pearls, a prayer for my patient. Please live. Surely, my judges wouldn't look this equable if she were dead? All the room settles for a moment around my fear, and my fear changes too. Oh, please don't let me be undoctored. Do not strike me off, erase me, make me nothing.

I was good at all those exams. I kept boxes of index cards, packed full of medical facts, all color-coded. And now I will prepare the ghosts of index cards in my mind. A pink for my patient. A blue for me. I will record only crucial facts since I know I cannot expect to catch every detail. With this wandering, this unraveling, there is only so much I can achieve.

The middle-aged woman, who reminds me of Boadicea, is a surgeon called Dr. Mansfield. She is to chair the four sessions which will define at least the next month, if not the rest, of my life. The guy is a GP, Dr. Garber. The lady in brown is Vivien from Occupational Health. She is like the court stenographer. With effort, I assimilate these words:

"...a complaint lodged last week with the General Medical Council by Joseph Jones, one of the anesthetic staff..." Joe? Who would have thought it? I assumed it was Frederick. I listen again. Her voice is clean as a wire. "...GMC contacted the Chief Executive of this hospital trust having accorded this complaint Stream 2 status."

I dip and I surface, down into myself and back into the room. I grasp what I can of what is being said.

"...been asked to assess this case locally. We, the panel, have been assembled by the Chief Executive for this purpose. We have all received training from the GMC. There is an additional member of the panel, not here today. This time next week, you will meet Dr. Gilchrist from our neighboring psychiatric unit. He will report back to us on his findings after that meeting. During the third session, we will concentrate on your recent performance as a doctor. In a fourth session, we will give our verdict. We have the facility to refer the case back to the GMC for reclassification as Stream 1 if things become too complicated or difficult for us to manage here. Or we may arrive at a decision ourselves about your professional future."

There is talk of bureaucratic bodies. The brown woman has to write fast to get down the National Clinical Assessment Service as well as the National Patient Safety Authority. They are the ones that have recommended my suspension from work until a conclusion is reached. I am afraid of these institutions, previously unheard of, now pitted against me. But I know that it is the people in front of me, these appointed colleagues from my own hospital, who hold the real power when it comes to deciding my fate.

Dr. Garber's voice comes low and I think of Julia and wonder how she might represent these two voices, the woman's and the man's, on a musical stave. But then I am all focus again because the soft GP is mentioning my girl, my woman, my patient, talking about her in the present tense, and the flood of relief to hear her spoken of in this way means I miss the first bit of what he is reading from the sheet in front of him. But, when I do listen, the medical language is like a balm. It is made of words I still trust:

"...was admitted to the ICU of this hospital straight from theater suffering the acute effects of major hemorrhage. E.S. required a transfusion of twelve units of blood in the first twenty-four hours. After two days of ventilation on the unit, a tracheostomy was performed and is still patent. The patient's main problems currently are disseminated intravascular coagulation and respiratory distress syndrome."

Alive, alive, thank God. Still alive, although of course she is far from safe. I watch the GP's face. He looks up at me and smiles.

"The good news is that her hemoglobin is... well, it's actually seven-point-nine," he says.

He places his hands in front of him on the desk and I hear a quiet tap as his wedding ring makes contact with its surface. His features are cast in shadow by the light from behind, but I know his face is a gentle one. And my patient is still alive.

"It's not such a bad result now, is it?" he says.

I was nine years old when my dad came home one day and announced that we would be moving to America for a few years. He was leaving the following month to get things ready, and my mum and sister and I would follow him a few weeks after that. With this one statement, he changed the course of my life.

The transformation in me began even before we left England. As soon as my dad arrived in our new home he began sending us parcels, each one contributing to the imagined scenery of the new life that awaited us. There were photographs of a cherry-red car, of sunshine on a pretty house and garden, of my dad smiling and wearing his first ever pair of blue jeans. And scratch-and-sniff stickers, each paper circle smelling of a foreign and wonderful junk treat—pizza, popcorn, bubble gum, Coke. Best of all was the package in which he sent my sister and me each a kazoo, a bizarre little plastic toy which, applied to the mouth, turned one's voice into a wonderful sonorous buzz. My mum was amazed to see me making so much noise on mine as I tootled away, all around the house.

When my dad met us off the plane, I saw the bright truth of the story his missives had told us. In the airport car park, the vehicle he led us to was enormous, and scarlet with bright yellow seats. The front part, where the adults sat, was a whole bench stretching across from steering wheel to passenger side, not like the frigid arrangement back at home. And there were two whole rows behind this for children, one facing forward and one backward so that you could choose whether to gaze into the future or look back into the past. My dad showed us all how the windows went up and down at the push of a button, and he blasted us with air conditioning and turned up the radio loud.

Our new house was on a main road, opposite one of the city's biggest hospitals. But it was set back behind a tall hedge so that once the car was in the driveway you could forget that you were really in the hub of a metropolis. Viewed from just inside this hedge, the house looked to me like something from a storybook. It was made of red brick, and it had a shiny tiled roof with a perfect little chimney, and a path covered in white gravel leading up to the door, which was glossy green with a brass knocker. Only the house number, on a matching brass plaque, reminded one by its four digits what an endless urban road we were on, for the character of the place was all intimacy. Flowers banked the gravel path and these same blooms filled bright window boxes outside each of the gabled windows.

My dad had arranged for my sister and me to sleep on the landing where he and my mother were, one of us on each side of them. I felt great pleasure at the glamorous prospect of having a whole room to myself. Dad had brought some familiar things over with him from England. I noticed straightaway the blue Picasso poster, which looked so pretty here on my new yellow walls, and one of my mother's colorful handmade quilts. My father had cozied my bed up in a corner of the room so that its head end was right next to a window through whose fly-netting I could look down on the cupcake-pink petals of a magnolia tree and, beyond it, the green slope of our new neighbor's miniature golfing range.

At the foot of the bed was an orange corduroy beanbag for sitting on. Against the facing wall, whose window looked out on the hedge and the main road beyond, I found a perfect bureau-style desk. The fact that it was made from real wood gave it a certain grown-up cachet, but it was child-sized. It had a curved rolltop and a small swivel stool, and two deep square drawers next to the space in which my legs would be tucked. Against the only remaining free wall my dad had put all my toys, the box of Lego, the red cot with the white rubber rim and my teddies.

He left me, jet-lagged, to settle into my new bedroom. Light fell on the pink carpet, and all around the room in rays. I put down my airplane bag, in which I had carried my books and crayons and favorite doll across thousands of miles. And I took off my shoes and started very slowly to walk barefoot around the edge of the circular rug at the center of the room, heel to toe, as if in miniature I were padding out the journey I had just made so fast and so massively, assimilating this transatlantic fact in my own little sphere of world, in my own new universe. And as I carefully trod, feeling the crushing of new plush beneath and between my toes, I allowed myself to unhinge from the distinctness of the new environment. I let my nine-year-old head loosen itself from the outside to fall back into the inside and, soundlessly to start with, I found myself chanting, "I am me. I am me. I am me," with only the keep-turning curve of the rug at my feet to look at. I kept going with this slow mind-spiral until I was saying the words right out loud, yet I was still so much inside myself that all at once I was afraid I might never get out again. I stopped sharply, to shake my head a bit, and looked around my new room and saw that it was beautiful and that I belonged in it. And I marveled at the fact that this journey, from one country to another, seemingly so accidental, so entirely out of my hands, could have made me feel suddenly and irreversibly so very important.

When I look up again, the room is full of sunshine. It frames my judges. I see the soft outline of the hair on their heads. Their faces are hard to make out, but I note that it is Dr. Mansfield who is talking now, asking me questions. I'm not sure when this happened, this change from the GP to her. She is inquiring about my choice of career. Were there any physicians in my family? That sort of thing. No, I answer her. I look over to the window. Somewhere, down below, I hear angry traffic. My judge's voice seems more distant than ever. I feel like I'm there but also not there. She is asking me about becoming a doctor. She wonders when I made that decision. Was I a

child? No, it happened later than that. I think that's what
I tell her.

At my new school, daily life was as far from what I'd
known as could be. No more the cold rough playground,
the crabby teachers, the sadness. This institution seemed
built for fun. It was mainly constructed of pale wood,
and decked out in primary colors. Signs above every
door reminded us that we were all "Welcome" and "Free
to be you and me."

My third-grade teacher, Mrs. Ranger, knew all about
me. On my arrival, she announced to the class, in an
excited voice, that everyone should stop their work at
the little round tables at which they sat in groups, and
go straight to the soft corner for show-and-tell. As she
did this, she clapped her hands together, the bracelets
on her wrists chimed, and her pearly fingernails made
me notice her matching pretty mouth. Everyone sat in a
horseshoe at Mrs. Ranger's feet and she settled on one of
the low chairs and held me next to her with her cool, soft
hands on my shoulders. She swept an approving glance
all the way along the row of children and told them it
was a wonderful day, for they were about to make a new
friend all the way from London, England. And then, one
by one, each child came up and stood before me and
said, "Hi, I'm Mimi" or "Hi, I'm Candy" or "Hi, I'm
Ned," until I had been talked to and smiled at twenty-
odd times, and each time I said "Hello" in return. I think
I uttered more greetings in one half-hour than I had in
my whole life.

At intervals in this introduction, Mrs. Ranger turned
me slightly towards her to check my expression then

21

back again to the open faces of my new friends. Sometimes, one of her hands lightly left my shoulder to stroke my hair as she spoke. She smelled of oranges and lemons.

Next, I was asked to speak a sentence or two about where I came from. I amazed myself by managing this easily, because it was my lovely new teacher who had requested it and because my new friends looked at me as if it was a natural thing to do. I didn't get further than the first few sentences, though, before the children all started clapping and squealing things like "Wow" or "That's so cute" just because of how I spoke. And my teacher didn't discipline this outburst: she joined in, laughing along so that I could see a single piece of gold twinkling at the back of her mirthful mouth.

By the end of my first semester I was taking my turn to stand in front of the class to recite the preamble to the Constitution, my famous accent already beginning to soften and the tremble in my voice came from pride now, not from fear. I could not believe in these first few months in my new home how easy it was to be happy, nor why it had taken so long for it to happen.

Mrs. Ranger did have a strict side. I saw her bring unruly boys quite close to her for a telling-off in her firm voice, and at these times her eyebrows would lower and her glossy hand would jut a finger out as she uttered some chiding sentence. But, even when she was formidable, her language seemed to reference the wholesome side of life. "Now don't you get fresh with me" was the severest thing I ever heard her say.

At the end of the day, all of us pupils sat chatting to each other, alongside our backpacks, in a corridor made of glass which let in the light of each intense season, waiting for one of the kindly teachers to announce through a megaphone which car was coming up the school's winding driveway to take us home.

There is a point in each of our lives when it seems that the real story begins, when we become the self that all our ensuing life somehow trails out from. This may just be the time, around three or four, when memory begins. But my birth, in this sense, occurred during one glowing American fall. This is when I became myself. The girl before this time is a shadow, like a soul who is practicing how not to become. She is the background, the hole in the fabric from which the real shape is cut.

Light empties from the room, as surprising as a sound. For a moment, everything goes quite dark, before the sunshine returns, playing on the windowpanes, casting a geometric map on the plain carpet. It glints off something on Dr. Mansfield's hands. I assume it must be a diamond until I see, as she passes leather folders along the table to her colleagues, that it is in fact the GMC badge on the front of one of the binders that has caught the light.

"I'd like to rule out a physical cause for what happened in theater, Nancy." Dr. Mansfield's two helpers open their files as she addresses me. "Were you unwell at the time, with anything at all, in the days leading up to the accident?"

I shake my head. She refers back to her notes. "And you don't have any medical or psychiatric history?" I wait for her to look up at me, then shake my head again.

"Okay. Well, I'm going to read out what I have here

about the events of that day. It's compiled from what others witnessed in theater—the anesthesiologist, scrub nurse, anesthetic assistant, you know. It's what happened from their point of view. And I want you to stop me if anything doesn't seem right. Okay?"

I nod but I don't get far. I sit very still in front of my judges but I only manage to hang on to what Dr. Mansfield says for a very short while.

America wasn't all rosy. A shiny girl I might now be, but I knew that the darkness that had seeped into me before our move from England, making me heavy as soil, was still at large. I sensed it at night when I heard the ambulances careening in and out of the hospital across the road, their lights making my whole room a ghoulish scintillation of red and blue. I felt it each time I walked past the vacant lot next to our house, a scrubland where poison ivy and goldenrod wooded out the sky, dwarfing even my parents, a place that my mother told me never to go because of dangers there; Baba Yagas and Jabberwocks, she said, not realizing I knew of worse things than these.

It was something to be able to walk past the vacant lot and not into it. That was an easy decision. But how was I to keep all the other threats at bay? How should I anchor the happiness that had come to me so surprisingly? I was tormented by this mystery and, not knowing what else to do, I resolved merely to walk away from all that was shaded or sad, to stick by glowing things. I kept on the sunny side of the road. I played with chirpy girls. And so it was, in what came with one such friendship, that I stumbled on the answer to the question that preoccupied me, learning that there was a better way to trick darkness than by just turning hopefully away from it.

One day, a new family moved to our street, into a house I hadn't noticed before, situated as it was at the far edge of the vacant lot, almost hidden within the jungle of rubbish and high weeds and wildness. Soon after their arrival, my mother and I were invited to go and have tea with our new neighbors. They had two daughters, a teenager and a girl just older than me. My mother told me that both girls had been adopted.

I could tell by the way she looked at me when she used this new word that the business of having parents who hadn't always belonged to you was not meant to be abnormal. I did not tell my mother that she was the only person I could ever imagine crawling in next to on a weekend morning, pushing my back up against her warm, soft scentlessness, just faintly picking up the smell of my dad's sweat on their green cotton sheets. I wouldn't have wanted to do this melting thing with any other woman.

The two sisters were starkly unmatched. My mother said this was because they had come from separate homes, where they had had different experiences. The elder one, Spencer, was an adolescent. She had a sad and textured face and I hardly ever saw her leave her bedroom. She must have done, though, because I heard that now and then she would jump from her bedroom window and break a leg or an arm on the concrete below. She never finished herself off, but was occasionally taken over the road to the hospital to be wrapped in plaster. The time my mum and I took her there, she was greeted by the nurses like a regular.

I wondered how Spencer had got the experiences which made her so forlorn, and how Victoria, the other sister—whose friendship I immediately craved—had come by hers, which made her so beautiful. And where I fitted in. Did a girl not have any say in how things turned out?

On that first visit to her house, I realized I had seen Victoria before. She had been standing beside the bus stop exactly halfway between her house and mine. My sister and I had been playing a spy game with the new walkie-talkie set we had been given for Christmas. This involved one of us sitting at the kitchen table recording information about people descending from the bus, dictated by the other one, who was usually parked at the end of the driveway. Each person we observed got an individual piece of paper, and we filed our descriptions away in a lever-arch folder which was brown with vicious corners.

I had experienced a strange thrill of gladness at being the person on the outpost that day. Usually I preferred being the amanuensis, because my writing was neater than my sister's and my powers of embellishment more advanced. I knew that a person had to be transmogrified for the written report, made slightly more significant than they really had seemed, or our game would collapse under its own mundanity.

But with Victoria, there was no need for flourishes. She was slim and strong. Her muscles had definition and I would soon envy the way she looked in exactly the same Speedo I felt so ungainly in. When I first saw her, she had on an emerald-green top made of Lycra with a deep V-neck and plunging back to match. I discovered later that this was actually a leotard. Over it, she wore a pair of old tracksuit bottoms and white Nike tennis shoes. One of her feet was pointed forwards, the other out at a marked angle, ballet-style. My eyes surveyed her: shoes, trackies, body like a snake in green, all the way up to her perfect blond head. She was the most compelling character study I had yet made in my antics with my sister. I actually wondered whether our game, previously so slack, had acquired some kind of momentum or point in it after all, for I felt an urgency and purpose in the way I examined Victoria, that strange greedy thrill of not knowing if a girl you observe is someone you want to be, to have, or to destroy.

A year or so later, I inherited the green leotard from Victoria. In a big bin bag of malodorous hand-me-downs, among all the grays, was a crushed little jewel of a green thing. My excitement at receiving this garment, which so emblematized my friend's great beauty, was matched only by my disappointment when I put it on one evening, alone in my bedroom, and confronted my jade body in the full-length mirror of my cupboard door. Looking at myself, my callow hope for glamour immediately dashed, I saw I could not escape myself. And though I was as dismayed as any girl who realizes she is not lovely, I was soon to discover that I had other strengths I could be proud of.

Victoria was a conventional girl. We played ponies. We made tiny, stapled storybooks and clothes for our dolls. We set up camp. This making of dens was probably my favorite activity: I liked establishing with my friend a cozy corner in a house which I found a little spooky. If our home was sun-dappled, hers was shrouded, a color chart of darks. And while ours was so tidy that when any of it was a mess it meant a family statement like "We've just had lunch" or "Dad's in the shower," theirs was chaotic. The kitchen surfaces were covered with stuff. The girls' rooms were like laundry cupboards, soft piles of clothes heaped on floors and beds and chairs. Toys were allowed to colonize spaces over time, and were never packed away.

What I enjoyed most was when my friend and I lay next to each other under a duvet in one of our makeshift camps, and she would tell me all about the weird stuff her older sister did. She said that Spencer had been a part of their family for just a few months and that her parents said it would take her time to settle in. That everyone needed to accommodate her behavior.

Most of these antics didn't amount to much. Spencer had shown Victoria how to make an earthy paste by mixing a few drops of water with soil and some extra-powerful ingredient such as her mother's Pert shampoo or a little shaving foam. This paste was to be applied to the cracks in the concrete next to the garage where the ants streamed, and Spencer enjoyed watching them drown in it. She also showed Victoria a book of black-and-white photos their father kept in his bedside table and insisted they look through them together.

But, one day, my friend told me about something that had happened over the weekend that had really scared her, an incident she had kept to herself. When their parents were out, Spencer had come into her room and asked if she'd like to do something cool. Victoria recognized her father's golf-ball key ring in her sister's palm and Spencer was shaking the bunch of keys in the air so that they danced and jangled.

The girls went down the stairs. Perhaps they taught kids to drive when they were really young in the home that Spencer had just come from, Victoria thought. Perhaps they'd just roll the car along the drive. Down and down they went, into the cool dark basement. Spencer headed for the door which led to the garage. They got into the car, with Spencer in the driving seat and Victoria where her mum usually sat, just as it should be. It was too dark to find the square button that opened the garage door, but Spencer must know where it was, for she had put the key in the ignition and started the car.

Victoria recognized the smell of the car smoke. It made her long for other smells. For leaves in the driveway, and chlorine, and the metal stink on one's hands after going on the climbing frame. But the car smell got stronger and the garage door didn't open. Victoria looked at Spencer and saw that her sister's eyes were closed and she had a special smile on her face, which Victoria had already learned to find scary. She told me that they stayed there like that until it was hard to see much in the garage even though the car windows were open. Then suddenly Spencer turned the car off and opened the garage door with the remote control, and they both watched as clouds billowed from the garage. Victoria said it reminded her of a genie, the way the poisonous smoke rushed out and up into the thin, blue air of their backyard.

The day after Victoria told me this story, she was due to come to my house to play. I had been thinking a lot about what she had told me, so when I heard the doorbell and went to answer the door, my heart thumped in my chest when I discovered it was Spencer standing outside. She told me her sister was ill with strep throat. That her mum had asked her to come and play instead and she had brought their swingball game over, which we could use in my backyard.

I felt disappointed and not a little afraid, but there seemed nothing for it but to invite Spencer in, then out of the back door into our garden where she began to set up the swingball. The garden sloped down a hill, but there was one small patch that was flatter than the rest where a tree had been felled ages ago. The old spiky bits from the sliced trunk, softened with time like driftwood, were covered with moss. On the steep gradient of the scraggy lawn, this old tree base was relatively flat so we thrust our swingball pole right through the middle of it. It lodged there surprisingly stiffly.

Spencer offered to stand down the hill a bit because she was bigger than me. And we began to play our game, like girls do, not competitively, but working together to see how many times we could hit the ball consecutively before one of us missed it—finding new patterns, hitting it directly back and forward or letting it swing right round before whacking it with the satisfying center of the plastic bat.

When we let the ball free to fly in its improbable circle through the sky, we loosened too as we beheld its graceful flight. I was happy to watch Spencer reaching high, her face lightening as she stretched up and out without inhibition to reach that lime ball with the blue bat. Then abruptly the moment was cut with a cry that I knew had nothing to do with the small effort of hitting the ball.

Spencer was sitting on the grass, leaning over her bare foot which she was holding shakily in her hand.

It was the first time I had ever seen someone else's blood. Across Spencer's fat white foot ran a bright-red line of about three inches with a thick piece of brown glass in the middle of the gash, poking upwards. It was a wound so severe that you could see the precise thickness of the skin and, beneath it, a pool of absolute redness which soon overflowed its bounds, trickling off Spencer's sole and into her hands as she sat palely holding it and staring at me.

The ball was swinging just a little now on its string. You could hear the click of the plastic loop banging against the metal spiral as it slowed down. I too felt a sort of swinging inside. A bit of a white sickness, but also a red sort of fulsomeness. The white feeling would have just kept me still, observing the moment. But the red feeling gave me a strong sense of purpose. I picked the glass gently out of the wound. Then I took off my T-shirt and I wrapped it around Spencer's bleeding foot and tied it. I put on my discarded flip-flops and ran to get my mother, relieved enough in my knowledge of her stoic nature to enjoy some excitement at the shocking news I was running to give her.

When my mum followed me back out to the garden, she untied the T-shirt on Spencer's foot to have a look at the wound, nodded quietly and retied it just as I had done, which was satisfying. We each took one of the bleeding girl's arms and led her to the car. And together we drove the fifty or so yards to the hospital over the road.

Spencer's mother was stuck at home with a feverish

Victoria, so my mum sat with her while her foot was stitched and I stayed in the waiting room. I didn't mind this, but I did resent the way the nurse kept bringing me toys. I knew I had not behaved like a child that afternoon. I had mastered a crisis. I had been calm and collected. Later, we went back to my house and Mum let us have Coke as well as Oreo cookies. When our neighbor came to pick up her daughter, Spencer piped up and said, "You should have seen Nancy. She was amazing! She totally looked after me," so that I got to feel the warmth of everyone's eyes on me. And I thought to myself that it hadn't been difficult at all, doing what I had done. I had loved coming to the rescue.

There is a clatter as Dr. Mansfield replaces her teacup on its saucer. She makes a tiny noise in her throat as if to acknowledge the mistake as she rights it. Is she embarrassed not to be in perfect physical control just because she is a surgeon? Or perhaps it's more of a female thing. That she feels un-dainty to have fumbled with fine bone china? Looking across the judges' table, I see there is a cup in front of each one of them. I don't know where the tea came from. I don't remember anyone bringing it in. I look around myself, down at my own ankles. It seems I haven't been given any.

Dr. Mansfield's eyebrows are raised and I realize I have missed something else. She repeats herself.

"Do you have any questions? Anything you want to add at this stage?"

"Nothing, ma'am," is my reply and I am glad to hear my voice at all. I have hardly used it during this hour. I have said so little since that day.

"Nothing?"

"Nothing."

All of them are looking at me now. Dr. Mansfield consults her bracelet watch and turns to me again. She leans towards me with her message. She uses her arms and her face together in a lively way to tell me not to be passive, that this is my time to stand up for myself. It's not what becomes of my patient that will make the difference. It's what I say in this room that counts. There is no more in me, though. I cannot muster another word. And so it is in silence that my first panel session comes to an end.

I leave the conference suite behind and re-enter the clinical part of the hospital. As carpet gives way to lino, I hear the sound of my footsteps again and I allow myself to exhale. My patient is still alive. I have not collapsed at the first hurdle. There is still something to play for.

I pass the surgical ward where I spent most of my internship year, and I remember how I learned to put in an IV there. A little further along the corridor, I take note of the tutorial room in which many of my undergraduate clinical exams took place. I walk out of the hospital and cross the road, heading for the bus stop.

A rubbish truck pulls up to the pavement and I wait while two men in green tabards load bags into its open back. One of them disappears from view, down to the basement of a terraced house. I can only see his arms as he chucks up his cargo. The other stands in the middle of the pavement, catching the sacks and dumping them in the back of the lorry. Two doctors, on their way to the Day Surgery Unit angle their way alongside the rubbish man, taking care not to brush against him, grimacing openly at the stink of refuse as they pass. I wait. When the last bag has been thrown up, I step forward. I feel the worker's eyes on me as I pass, but I do not meet them with my own.

My bus arrives and I have only just found a seat on the empty upper deck when my phone begins to ring. I pull it from my rucksack and peer at its screen, more out of curiosity than with any real intention of speaking to anyone. But I press the green button straightaway when I see it's my sister calling me.

"Julia."

"How did it go?"

"Well, she's still alive."

"Oh, thank goodness. Thank God! How was it, though?"

"How was it? I don't know. It was fine. No, it wasn't fine. It was horrible. I had so much that I wanted to say. But I just...I don't know. I just didn't say it. Or I didn't say it right. I didn't say enough of it right—"

"But you managed to hold it together?"

"Yeah, I guess I did. Is that something?"

"Nancy, that's the main thing. It's all you needed to do. All the rest will take care of itself. But they—"

"They told me the rubric of the thing. Asked me a few questions. And they went over what happened in theater. Which was awful, hearing it aloud like that. Anyway, the next session's with a bloody psychiatrist. I'm already dreading it. But enough. How's Dad? It's been two weeks now since I saw him. I feel terrible."

"He's fine, Nancy, absolutely fine. We all are. And you know I'm happy to cover your visits for a while. God knows, I owe you. So what I want to know is this.

Will you come and stay the weekends with us while this whole thing is going on? I'd love it. We all would."

"Well, all right. I mean, yes please, I'd love to, if you're sure it's okay. I'll tell you something, though. There is one good thing about this whole business. I've actually got time to do some studying now. I'm going—"

"You know what, Nance? I actually don't want to hear about your work. I'm absolutely sick of it, and all the trouble it's caused. Sorry, but can we talk about something else?"

"Okay, Jules. But let me ask you something. You know when we were kids? Do you remember that feeling of being little, when all we did was charge about and get filthy? And being a wild thing was totally okay? Was that just in America, or were we still like that after we came home? I was just trying to figure it out. When was it suddenly not acceptable to be doing all that stuff?"

"Oh, Nancy. For goodness' sake!" is all my sister says. "Look, I'll call you again tomorrow. Lots of love." And then she hangs up.

I know Julia is upset with me. But I don't stop to think of her in that moment. Because there it is, for the first time in years, the memory of child-passion. Heavy as a stamp in my mind. Still a bright clean memory, despite its sordid sequel.

I am twelve. We are coming to the end of our stay in America. During our last summer we are visited by family friends from London. I hardly remember them but when they arrive I find that their boy, who is a few years older than me, has become beautiful. I stand in front of him and think straightaway that Tom is the best boy I have ever seen.

My sister is a delicate thing who likes to play with dolls. And Tom's brother has gray skin, and only wants to be fast at solving the Rubik's Cube, his wrists clicking, his fingers flicking at its colored squares. So Tom and I go outside. And everything waits for us. The creek at the base of the yard, and trees as giant as all American things, and the forbidden vacant lot.

Every summer's day leading from that first one is for throwing ourselves against the world. In my evening bath, I lie in mire, counting my injuries, pleased to see fresh ones replace those that are healing, knowing that Tom is somewhere on the other side of the door, not far away. And he will be there again tomorrow.

Towards the end of the vacation, we all go together to the Blue Ridge Mountains in Virginia. The outdoors is even grander there, its expansiveness bringing us closer together as we dash at it. The hugeness of this world makes us more tired than we were in my backyard. So that we start to take a rest even quite early in the day, perhaps before we are really tired, our puffing and panting and finding a log to sit on not without a histrionic element.

In the final week, the grown-ups suggest the four of us kids might like to camp out for a night. The dads help us find a good spot, on a ledge near the top of the mountain, a mile or so from our log cabin. The boys nick two bottles of beer from a dusty fridge in the garage of the house, stashing them in a nearby tree stump for our night out.

There are two tents, one for my little sister and me,

one for Tom and his brother Richard. We pitch them both, and all get into our sleeping bags to make a show for Julia of the evening's fun being over. Once she is asleep next to me, the boys go off to get the beer, taking the big torch and leaving me the small one. I know they'll be away half an hour since the booty tree is quite a distance from where we are camping.

When the boys leave, I am spooked. It's a blustery night. The shape of the empty tent nearby looks scary, its triangular outline harsh, its billowing fly-sheet ghostly. The sheer face of the mountain opposite is luminous and rises steeply above where I lie. But it is not these things, really. It is that Tom is gone and I am still there. The gentle breathing of Julia sleeping next to me offers no comfort. It is the sound of my own softness.

I am also having one of my first ever periods. I have brought sanitary napkins with me in my rucksack and plastic bags and, knowing how hard it will be to look after myself discreetly when Tom and his brother come back, I force myself out into the wide night to change my napkin. The angled focus of the torch I lay at my feet, and the swishing of the bag I have under my shoe in the wind, and the very fact of having to negotiate barely understood genitals in the open blackness of outside intensify my fright. I am snugly in my sleeping bag, heart thumping, dressed again, when they return. Each carries a bottle of beer to avoid clinking and their spirits are high. I could cry with how glad I am to see them again.

We find the edge of the mountaintop and make it our seat. We're still near the tents so that we will hear my sister if she wakes. We love our high lookout, without feeling its treachery. Tom sits in the middle. The boys must have swigged some of the beer on their way back to me, for the first bottle is soon empty. One of them throws it behind us, and I hear its glassy thud on the ground and know by our laughter, which is not hushed now, that it is happening, just as we fantasized it would, the preposterous effect of this drink on us—setting me up for a habit of thinking, for years after this, that being drunk is the only possible way to do what I am about to do. We pass the second bottle along, backwards and forwards, but more slowly now. Every time I tilt my head back to sip starrily, there is a wider strange tipping, and I want to sit next to Tom, here on this ledge in the darkness, forever.

The boys are hearty to start with, but Richard's laughter soon becomes querulous. Next, he is standing right out on the precipice, a dark star wavering against the blackberry night. He exclaims that if he jumped we wouldn't care, that we just want to be together. And it is true, I think, it is true. Go away, go far away, I wish in my head, and I say nothing and nor does Tom.

It is no time before Richard goes off in a huff to his tent. We hear him zipping it shut. As soon as we are by ourselves, Tom asks to kiss me. No one will ever ask me this so courteously again. His face is like ice cream in the moonlight. And I swear to God that grown-ups are wrong to think we can know nothing of such things at our age, because this is the kissing against which all the other kissing in my life should be measured.

Tom is only fourteen so I am amazed by his hard arms, his rough cheek. I immediately feel more solid and true because I am wrapped in Tom and he is not just a boy. There is no taste to us at all. We kiss and talk, as if about the beach. The words are just the words. They do not suggest we are making a mistake. The only limit is the sanitary napkin, all bunched up in my jeans, which is warm, not just with the effect of Tom, but with the harsh fact of my period. It reminds me that there are edges to this night.

When we return to the house the next morning, I expect our parents to comment on what is right in front of their eyes. I want everyone to know. I feel we should be fed a celebration breakfast. But they completely ignore how things are. Our experience is given no adult meaning. It has no currency at all, then or later. So, as we write to each other for months after that bright night, even as we name our love, we use the word furtively like stealers and half cheats. Then we fall out of touch, although the memory of that night sustains me throughout a whole adolescence.

My journey home takes no time. There's hardly any traffic. I get off the bus and head for the building in which I have had a studio apartment ever since I started to earn a doctor's salary. I let myself in with the fob and am greeted by a security guard, sitting at the front desk. Behind him, a screen shows a view of corridors, all clean and empty, stretching this way and that towards multiple flats, all decked out in the modern style. I walk past the hideous blue sofa and armchairs that form a reception area, and make for the lift.

Two minutes later, I am opening the door to my little flat. I scoop up a pile of mail, hold the fire door so that it closes quietly behind me, and go straight over to my desk, which occupies the best position in my all-purpose room next to the window. As usual, the flat is too hot, baked from all sides by other people's radiators. I throw open both windows, and spread my mail on the desk in front of me before sitting down. Facing me, across a space of about forty feet, are the five identical windows of the flats on the other side of the building. Beneath these, four longer windows announce the more generous flats on the floor below. And at ground level is a paved courtyard with trees growing in among the stones and a bench or two for sitting on, on an afternoon like this one.

My parents wrote to me every week when I was at boarding school. Not just a single letter between them, but one each. But gone are the days when I might search in a pile of mail for something as lovely as a colored envelope inscribed with my name. The first thing I open is a photocopy of an article Frederick must have thought would be of interest, and which he has asked his secretary to send to me. It's about teenage pregnancy. Why don't girls simply avail themselves of our wonderful free contraceptive services? the author inquires. I tire of the theme quickly and put the paper down. I angle my chair so that I am looking, not at the brick wall opposite but up to the left, where someone in a high-up flat has decked their balcony with tubs and pots, and greenery reaches up into the London sky. A woman is sitting out there on a deck chair, painting her nails.

The fact is, it's not as simple as that. Seeking out contraception requires some kind of sense of self. And a girl's identity doesn't stick fast, does it? It isn't a case of finders keepers. You don't get to hang on to your confidence just because you've worked hard to earn it.

DIRTY WORK

*   *   *

I had a nasty shock starting boarding school in England after more than three years of relative educational freedom in the States. For a few months, the world felt topsy-turvy before I righted myself to the view that everything that had been deemed important on that side of the Atlantic was disapproved of on this. Being myself was no longer an important mission. It was time to fit in.

Quickly I learned that my days of getting dirty were over. My male classmates were given boilersuits to put over their uniforms after class. Get muddy wearing. Put holes through. Ride go-karts in. While the other girls jumped rope, I studied the boys with envy. In America, I would have been playing alongside them. Within weeks, my expectations had shifted, and my sole hope in watching them was to be watched in return.

Twice a week, they marshaled us for a shower. A matron blew a tubular whistle, like the ones you get with a policeman's costume, and we would line up at the dormitory door. Then we followed whichever unenticing Pied Piper was on duty that evening, down two flights of stairs to the subterranean shower room. There we stood in line without talking.

When you got to the front, you stepped into the shower bay among the other washing girls. You got wet and soaped yourself. All over your body, which I had never done at home, which I had not been taught was imperative. The matron had to approve of how soapy you had made yourself before you were allowed to rinse off and finish your shower. The two baths in the room were only for birthday girls.

I did okay at keeping clean. The punishments I got

were for not being quiet enough. I talked after lights-out, and I sniggered during meals. I whispered in chapel and I muttered to myself. For these infractions, I was sent on runs or made to learn psalms. Once, to my secret pleasure, I was instructed to wash and shine all the test tubes in the science labs. Little did they know how much I loved that acrid place, where sunshine caught the angles of metal and glass, where my only companion for the afternoon was the furious axolotl, sitting palely in his tank.

And then I learned what it is to really talk out of turn. One early summer, in a new dorm with five other girls which looked out on the playing fields, I observed something unusual. After rounders every day, we would change out of our gym clothes back into our uniforms and, since our cupboards were next to the window, this was where we often stood. No boys walked nearby since their games took place on the other side of the school. But, every day, one of the French teachers would take what seemed a long detour from where he taught cricket, to pass right by our window. And at exactly the same point in his walk, coming round a corner, he would look up at us as we undressed.

We were young, but we noticed. And one day, in high spirits but without thinking, seeing this middle-aged man look up just as three of my friends had removed their Aertex shirts, I opened the window and called out a single word before ducking down behind the radiator out of view. My voice sounded much louder than I had intended. My friends stopped giggling.

Five minutes later, the head matron appeared at the entrance to our dormitory. Her face was puce. She asked which girl had shouted from the window. With fear's almost genital lurch, I stepped forward. She took my arm and we walked, in plain view, across the school together. We passed by all the girls' dormitories. We looped in between Ping-Pong tables, where boys stopped their play. We went by the chapel and the classrooms and on into the mahogany-paneled part of the school that parents so admired.

Finally, we reached the entrance to the headmaster's office, with its door that stretched all the way up to the ceiling. Here I waited beneath the portraits of the headmaster's predecessors. After a while, I was summoned into a long room, which took me ages to compass. The headmaster sat behind his desk, legs crossed, strict as any father but twice the size. On the desk in front of him was a huge dictionary, not one bit like the ones in the English classroom.

"Show me" was all he said. He uncrossed his legs. I stepped forward, the tiny print dancing and forming prisms in my eyes. I saw the nefarious word I had called from the dormitory window again and pointed at it. He took the book back from me and, not looking down at it again, spoke. "Pervert," he said. "A person who changes their religious conviction."

After leaving the headmaster's study, I was sent to an empty classroom where I wrote out the definition of the word *pervert* two hundred times, lest I ever misunderstand its meaning so grossly again.

I look back at my desk, at the remaining mail. There is a council tax bill, which I put into an empty plastic tray marked "To do." The other bits of post relate to my work. There is a thank-you letter from the organizer of the Battle of Ideas, praising me on the recent talk I gave. There is something from the Pro-choice Alliance and an envelope marked with the Catholics for Choice insignia. A Technicolor image of a fetus at about twenty weeks' gestation announces itself immediately to my seasoned eye as antiabortion propaganda rather than information on advances in ultrasound imaging. I fold it carefully in two, so that the picture is on the inside, and slot it in between discarded envelopes in my wastepaper basket. Lastly, I pick up the latest issue of *Abortion Review,* tear it from its thin plastic wrapper and unfold it.

The woman on the balcony gets up from her chair. She fans her fingers out and blows absently on her nails. Then she looks directly at me. Out of habit, I slide my hands over the front of the journal lying on my desk. I've got used to doing this, covering my reading matter, obscuring its identity even in circumstances when someone would need X-ray vision to see what is in front of me. Some might call it shame. And maybe it's true. Perhaps my operating room is a dreadful place for a person to end up. But what would happen without people like me? What path, I wonder, apart from celibacy, is a girl meant to tread, if she is to avoid catastrophe? How on earth is she to negotiate the minefield of puberty and adolescence?

Soon after arriving at my English school I started to go out with a boy in my class in whom I had no sexual interest. This was a pity. There was a Nigerian boy in the year below whom I would have loved to wrap myself up in, but he wore Pringle jumpers and had odd friends.

By comparison, everyone thought Nick was cool and he liked me, so there was nothing more to be considered. Other than the fact that I was lagging behind most of the self-respecting girls in my class in terms of achieving the milestones of sexual accomplishment. And I needed to address this.

Nick and I would sit together in lessons, clasping and reclasping hands under the table. Sometimes we went for walks in break-time or after supper, getting far enough away from the penumbra glare of the school to find a gate or wall that we could lean against for kissing. But it was winter, and dark and perishing. There was nowhere to lie down and teachers roamed the grounds. I had no idea how I was meant to graduate to the expected level of sexual prowess for a girl in my year.

And then the perfect occasion presented itself. In the Christmas holidays, my friend Lucy's mother organized a sort of dance, and all the pupils in my year were invited. My own mother accepted an invitation for me to stay with this family over the weekend of the party and gave my friend's mother money to take me dress-shopping, with a quite specific brief. Ignorant of it, as usual, I was grateful to be in such safe sartorial hands. As long as I looked exactly the same as everyone else, I would be fine.

However, I had not bargained for the existence of a shop like Laura Ashley. Lucy and I were led by her mother straight to a railing on which hung a long row of dresses in fruity hues, with fitted bodices and puffy sleeves and sashes. Dresses that already had a shape, which they held on their rails, a shape into which any girl might be pressed, losing her own form, in order to make do. Dresses which looked like girls without heads.

Lucy seemed quite comfortable. There was no question of looking in any other shop. Her mother even ruled out allowing us to choose black, so we left that place an hour after entering it with matching watered silk girl-gowns in feverish colors, my friend's a burnt orange, mine magenta.

I had never bought a dress before so I didn't realize the occasion was meant to be pleasurable. Still, I was able to suppress my dislike of what I now owned because of my relief that I'd be wearing exactly what I should be. But in the forty-eight hours in between taking the dress back to Lucy's house and having to put it on, my horror found a more concrete focus. Which was how absolutely disgusting I would look when I arrived at the dance and Nick saw what I was wearing. He who had desired me as I felt I really was, sulking in sundry jeans and old-man-style cardigans.

Caught in between these two hard facts—the necessity for the magenta dress and my loathing of it as imagined through the eyes of my boyfriend—my teenage brain could compute only one solution: to wear jeans underneath my dress, rolled up just high enough for Lucy's mother not to spot them at my dimpled ankles. Did I foresee an occasion when, with one upward flourish of a hideous skirt, I could apologize for my false self by revealing my jeaned authenticity to Nick? Or did I just want the reassuring feeling of my own second skin, the softened denim rounding my adolescent butt? Either way, this small subterfuge enabled me to leave my friend's house, get in the car and go to the party.

Nick was there when we arrived, standing slightly apart from a group of girls from my year, who, I was relieved to see, were all wearing the same hideous frocks Lucy and I had on. I didn't feel any particular desire when I saw him, but I liked the way he looked in slim snaky trousers with rebel boots. And his hair was all over the place.

He gave no sign of recognizing my awkwardness, but smiled me over, and straightaway scooped from his pocket a handful of Smarties which he half emptied into my palm, saying, "Best of five, then?" He tossed the sweets up in the air one by one and caught them in his mouth, ducking like a footballer leaning to head a ball before tipping his head back to snap the colored confection he was catching there.

I followed suit with my Smarties, keeping very still as if to show I could better him in style; in fact not wanting to swirl my pink dress around me, not wanting to reveal the sheer mass of the gaudy drapery, preferring to keep my crocodile-snapping mouth and girl's gullet the focus of his attention. "Five all," he concluded cheerfully, and this head-tipping tournament was the only feint we needed before Nick leaned over to say, "I've got some smokes. Come on." No one watched us leave.

Outside was cold and black and smelled of stars. Nick gave me his jacket and we found somewhere just a little wet to sit. The jacket touched the ground at my sides, its length making gaps between me and it, and this gave me the idea to roll and scrunch my skirt as you do with sheets you are bundling into the dirty laundry. And so I packed away the pink swathes of my dress and positioned the skirts under its flaps. Folding the lapels, I drew them to my neck to cover all sights of pink bodice. I accepted the cigarette that Nick had double-lit with his own, tasting his sweet flob on the filter, just as I beheld myself successfully de-pinked, the denim and dark jacket making me feel quite myself again for the first time that evening.

Did he sense this thrill I had at seeing myself? Did he interpret my skirt-shifting differently before he saw I only meant to reveal my jeans below? Was it the sight of these jeans or just the fact of sex that made him turn straight to my mouth, so that his smoke soon came from my nose in the dark night, my own cigarette burning in my still hand, an ashy tower rising steadily from its glowing tip?

It would be wrong to say that kissing was all I wanted. A lie to pretend my mind didn't beseech his hands to find their way to the warm, soft interior of his jacket where parts of me, at least, were a little grown up by now. We made the best of things, although the bodice of my dress was so tight that Nick couldn't get his hands into it, and the folds of my dress kept unraveling around my jeans.

The occasional reappearance of parts of this dress and the dreadful swirling and rummaging in the voluminous pink skirts made it hard for me to enjoy myself, so I decided to just get on with what I had to do. I had to be able to claim I'd done it when I returned to school the following term.

In the loamy dark, it was not Nick that guided my hand to his penis, but my own strong sense of social duty. Nor did he make me continue once I realized what hard work it was. He did not suggest it, any more than anyone at my new school had told me the things I had later found to be crucial: that I might save myself from near-inevitable social exile by coming back from the Christmas holidays with the right trainers. That it would help if I could sing along to David Bowie instead of Supertramp. That I should learn how to inhale a cigarette. That I should own clothes that someone else might want to borrow. That I should have the boldness that comes from these things.

When Nick removed his hand from my pants that night and put it over mine to help me with what I couldn't manage myself, I was simply grateful to him. And when, for the first time in my life, I saw sperm, on Nick, on me, in the air, all over the quiet folds of my darkened dress, I was only partly concerned about how I would clean myself up; mainly I was relieved that this pursuit was finally over. We picked our barely smoked fags off the ground next to us and as I relit mine I noticed the faint bitterness in its taste.

I have no job to go to, and snow falls on London. It stops, only to start up again. I lie in bed well past six, looking up into the sky, thinking of my patient. Anxious that the slow-falling processes in her body, the drifts of electrolytes across cell membranes, the sweep of inflammatory mediators and catecholamines, the piling up of work on vital organs, should go in her favor and not against her. To bear her towards life and not death. And there is nothing I can do.

I wander to the corner shop for bread and milk each morning. Everyone is caught up in the weather. The radio says we should all stay at home. The pretty lady on morning TV continues to sit on her red sofa in lovely dresses. And it is as if the world has stopped for my patient, has gone stock-still for me in my vigil. I go home with provisions and review my anatomy, to try and improve myself. I relearn venous drainage of the pelvis, innervation of the pudendum, lymphatics of the lower limb. I study the blood supply to the uterus and so anatomize my own failure, reminding myself of where all that blood I spilled came from. From the uterine artery, the arcuate and azygos vessels. Leaching onto hands and legs and floor and drapes and around everything.

Halfway through this first week off work, I wake knowing I cannot lie around anymore. I realize I'm not allowed into the hospital, that this is what it means to be suspended from my work. But, nonetheless, I long to be near my sick patient. I should be there to look after her, whatever has gone wrong. I kick the duvet off my legs and put on black tracksuit bottoms and a jumper. I hang my ID badge, on its tiny baubled chain, around my neck and zip my coat on top of it. I put my rucksack on my back and grab the bicycle lights from where they have lain untouched for a week, on their shelf below the telephone.

I take the lift to the ground floor, and walk along the deserted communal corridor to the exit. I step out into the cold dawn. I hear the quiet bitching of the trees, and see the stain of night around the square, and feel the scrutiny of blank-windowed cars. Only the smell of damp tarmac, always my mother's favorite, reassures me that this is not really the witching hour, but morning coming, just around the corner.

Cycling fast, I reach the hospital in no time. Snow ices the roofs of houseboats in the wharf and, under a mauve

sky, the river runs green beside me as I go. I lock my
bike as usual on the second bar from the right. I ascend
the steps towards the towering main doors of the hospital, within which two normal-size doors have been cut.
I step, with utter gladness, from the cold blue day into
the warm city of the hospital's interior, with its welcome
view of multicolored signage and light-glare and hospital shopfront and gleaming floor and the static prickle of
central heating on full. I head straight for the Intensive
Care Unit, where all my thoughts lie with my ailing patient. I know I am not allowed to go to her, so do the
next-best thing and find the closest bench I can to sit on.
The woman I have harmed cannot be more than a few
meters away from me. I feel my heart beat hard in my
chest, and I think of her heart. I pray for it.

A thin patient with a jaundiced face and bright yellow
eyes wheels his drip stand past me, on his way to the
smoking area. A man rolls a trolley of newspapers past
me towards the hospital shop. A young black man, his
face heavy with disappointment, clanks sanitary napkin
bins out of the women's loo at the top of a small ramp
near where I sit. Waste pokes from the top of the bins
and bloodstains are visible against the gray plastic. He
stops and turns to me, but I look away.

And then doctors and nurses arrive in groups and the
hospital begins to put on its face for the world, and I
know that, however much I wish I could keep my vigil
up all day, I can't afford to be discovered here loitering.
I go out through a different exit so I can see more of this
place that is my home. I walk past the canteen where I
always have my bacon butty after a night on call, and
past Endoscopy. And near the room with the flower sign,

which is not actually a florist's but a place where you go if you are going to have a colostomy and want a nurse to talk to you about it and comfort you. And past the long, wide corridor which leads to the ob-gyn wards, my very own quarters. I pause there and look down the corridor, wishing that doing this would tell me something, before leaving the hospital to collect my bike and return to where I live.

WEEK TWO

Day breaks on a Saturday at my sister's. I can't remember the last time I even noticed the weekend. The house is still, the sky and sea are one darkness outside the window. Straightaway I scan myself, my nightmind, and am relieved that I have had no bad dreams. No fetus dreams, baby dreams, Lady Macbeth–style dreams.

I sit up in bed and gather the pillows behind me, push others under my knees. Outside, the wild world is not declaring more than its simplest layers. Garden, wall and stones form a slab, and everything above this is sea and sky, though all I have to tell me which is which is the occasional stripe of wave brightness cutting across my sight line where I had imagined the horizon belonged. The morning is so thick that even Nab Tower, with its usual rounding blink, is invisible in the distance.

When I wake in London, I look at wall. Here, every ten seconds, there is change. I close my eyes and count. I open them and see the discs of groin posts peeping out from the sea. The next ten seconds bring a man with three dogs to the top of the beach. He bends to release them from their leads and all four take off, running down over the crest of the pebbles, out of view.

Morning arrives with each second. The house creaks above me and I hear through the walls Julia and Mark talking as they move about their room. And I wish I had this. I come out from my cocoon and shuffle over to the window. Then I hear my sister rebuking her son. "Leave Nancy alone. Let her, at least, get some sleep."

When I push the window open minutely against the weight of the wind, the wet hits my face, and the blare of the sea, one solid sound, overwhelms all else; drowns out domesticity so that I am back out there at large, with everything that has gone awry, and a young woman whom I might have killed, who may in fact be dead by now. May have stopped breathing in any of these instants. Go tell Aunt Nancy, go tell Aunt Nancy, go tell Aunt Nancy the old gray goose is dead.

I pull the window rubber shut and, just like that, I am back in this home, a part of it. I know this because my sister, with a softer voice now, is saying, "Well, all right then, I'll make you a cup of tea to take in to her."

When the weekend is over, Julia drives me to the station. We don't talk much. I look out of the window and consider whether it's worth getting cross with her. I imagine a possible, righteous script. I thought I was coming to stay with you so I could rest. And then you send me scurrying around for two days doing all your errands. I listen to my sister whistling softly, and try to identify her tune, which wraps itself around me. I unwind the car window a fraction so that I can smell the air off the sea. I think of the loose clasp of weeds in my fingers as I pulled them from the vegetable beds. Picture the small pile of flints I cleared from the soil. Recall the gentle toil of reading bedtime stories to my sister's children.

By the time we reach the car park, I have forgotten my irritation. I am even happy to indulge my sister, to listen to what passes for her homily. Don't squander the interview. Be confident, not tricksy. It's going to be fine. That sort of thing. Her words don't amount to much but I want to stay with her nevertheless, to keep in the orbit of her smell, to try and locate my mother in her eyes. My dear, sweet sister. And then, just like that, we're not together anymore. I don't immediately find a seat on the train, but keep looking out of the window. I imagine Julia driving away, but only for as long as I can see her car on the wet road as my train cuts across it. This is the limit of my imagination, then I am back in my own thoughts again.

I reach London with three hours to spare before the start of my second panel session. I know what I need to do. I get home as fast as I can and don't even bother to unpack. I pull out the stepladder, then rummage around in the top cupboard where I keep all my medical books, and finally manage to locate my old psychiatry folder. I make tea and toast and set up camp on the floor. I search through tons of files and books. I had forgotten just how complicated taking a psychiatric history is, all the different sections of it, all the areas of inquiry necessary to make an assessment of the vulnerable mind. I reacquaint myself with the rubric so that I will know my way around the diagnostic template that is about to be applied to me. I lick butter from my fingers and read about the mental state examination, take note of the fact that the doctor assessing me will be performing one of these as he goes, looking for signs of agitation, too much or too little eye contact, a pathological posture, an abnormally flattened or elevated mood. It's a minefield, but I hope it won't be such a daunting one if only I can work out where to find the explosives.

The problem is that all of this only helps me up to a certain point. The point at which I pack my books up and leave my flat behind. Because it is one thing to sit alone and make sense of what is about to happen, and quite another to hurtle towards this fate in the great outdoors. I don't have long to wait, but by the time my bus comes I have already had a couple of layers of confidence jostled away from me. And it doesn't matter that I find a seat right at the front so that I can enjoy the feeling of disappearing into trees as the bus pushes past low branches. After half an hour has gone by, I have been harried by the cacophony of so many others' conversations, by such a multitude of smells, such a swarm of coats and elbows, that half my composure has abandoned me.

When I step off the bus, near the hospital, and head towards the building in which the psychiatrist must already be waiting by now, I already feel I am under interrogation, under the cosh of my own neurotic mental inquiry, as if the official one I am about to face were not quite enough to contend with.

How has it come to this? How could you have ended up in this state, Nancy? Questions beleaguer me. What kind of human being performs abortions for a living? What sort of woman are you? Why did you end up doing this job? Can such a thing happen by accident? What female, in her reproductive prime, would actually agree to do this? A ruthless one, surely. A brutal one, no doubt. Quite out of the blue I think of the girl at school whom no one wanted to be friends with anymore. I remember her crying in the loo next to mine and how I crept away from her lest I became infected by her lack of popularity. I remember pushing my sister over in the mud in our backyard in America. I also remember the sound of a patient's tears.

Michael Hanforth was the golden boy of general surgery. We all knew him. There wasn't a single one of us who didn't, from medical student to top-dog specialist. And we all wanted a piece of him. This young buck walked so fast along the corridors that his bosses had to break into a trot to keep up with him on a ward round. Everyone wanted to sleep with him. All the nurses and physical therapists and medical students. All of us. I wish I could say that I was different but I was mad about him just like everyone else, desperate to be in his tutorial group, to have the benefit of his study notes, to own even a shadowy piece of the Hanforth magic.

I never was one of his students, though. Which was why I felt as if all my ships had come in when, one day, I was suddenly asked if I could go down to help out in a particularly busy general surgery clinic, a clinic being presided over by Dr. Hanforth.

I had no foolish ambitions. I was thrilled just to be helping on the sidelines and didn't imagine there would be any occasion to talk to or impress my surgical hero face-to-face. I worked hard all afternoon, taking blood, removing stitches, looking for X-rays. Then, towards the end of the afternoon, one of the nurses asked me to see a lady who was waiting in the treatment room to have her sutures taken out following an operation she'd had the week before.

I don't remember what surgery this middle-aged lady had undergone. She was lying behind a green curtain and as soon as I came into the room she hitched up her sweatshirt to reveal her abdomen. I guessed it might have been emergency surgery for an infection of some kind because what held this woman together was not the neat row of metal staples I was used to seeing, but something that looked like a plastic shoelace, crisscrossing her middle.

This green binding, the caliber of a drinking straw, had been fed through the open edges of the wound running from her chest to pubis about as many times as a shoelace would pass through the eyelets of a Converse baseball boot. But the thick stitch didn't sit loosely there. The skin of the patient's abdomen had healed enough to clasp each part of the tether in place, growing snugly around the plastic and hugging it. And the whole area was red with the effort of healing, with the hectic activity of inflammatory mediators rushing to the site of recent injury.

She didn't flinch as I approached her, gloves on. I was

pleased I looked so authentic. But as soon as I gave one end of the plastic suture a tug with a pair of surgical clips her hands fell reflexively onto mine to stop my efforts, which she clearly found uncomfortable. Gingerly, I tried another twitch before excusing myself to find whichever fellow was in clinic that day. I regretted having to disturb whoever this might be. The usual unfair pile of notes was stacked up outside their room, representing all the patients they still had to see, their own quota plus any extras the specialist could justify palming off as beneficial to their training.

When I knocked on the door a man answered, "Come in," and I recognized Dr. Hanforth's voice. I put my head round the door, and he beckoned me in, saying, "Have a seat. I'm just finishing my dictation." His manner was level, and I admired this, the democracy of his approach. I had already become so used, as a medical student, to being treated like the scum of the earth.

The letter he spoke into his Dictaphone came in clean short phrases. He did not need to flick the machine on and off or rewind. And then Dr. Hanforth placed the machine lightly on his desk and put the patient notes he had been looking at in a trolley beside him. He allowed himself one backward stretch, arms behind his head, sunbathing style, before settling forward again and asking, "What can I do for you?"

I told him who I was and what I was struggling with. He got up, ushering me out of the room before him as I finished my explanation, which I tried to make as practical and short as I could, wanting to please him, not unaffected by his straight-backed masculinity.

On entering the cubicle where I had left my patient,

Dr. Hanforth asked the lady, who was lying just as I had left her, for some details about her operation. She seemed more nervous than before, responding perhaps to his palpable seniority. Yet although she spoke to him she looked at me, seeking encouragement from my comparatively more familiar face. I knew it was mean of me, but I slightly resented this. I was nearly a doctor now, and wanted her to see me as his ally rather than hers.

Without waiting for her to finish speaking, Dr. Hanforth picked up the metal clips from the steel table where I had discarded them. He rolled backwards and forwards on his heels. He inspected the clips minutely and this surprised me because it struck me as rude, the scrutiny of his eyes combined with the nonchalance of his heels. I think his attitude made our patient apprehensive, for she fixed her gaze on me, causing me to look at my feet.

But then I did look up because abruptly the lady stopped talking and I heard her gasp. The sound made me feel bad before I even knew what had happened. Then I saw that my senior colleague had roughly pulled the first loop of the stitch from the patient's abdomen, transforming her face from placid to tearful in an instant. I wondered at how active the nasolacrimal gland could be to produce tears so briskly. I had always witnessed this process as being preceded by a slow welling.

I looked back and forth between Dr. Hanforth and the supine woman, the only way, without insubordination, that I could draw his attention to the distress he must surely have noticed he was causing. I saw the clips, bloodied at their jaws, moving straight to the second coil of suture. But on he went. And on.

With every length of stitch that he pulled out I caught

my breath, and with each of his emphatic arm move-
ments, a new personal feature of my patient leapt out
at me. Tug: pink lipstick, applied for the doctor's eyes.
Yank: necklace and matching bracelet, both in fine gold
braid. Pull: the heels of practical shoes, worn down on
one side. I dared not look at the face of the man beside
me, knowing I would find it as smooth as ever, sure now
that he was ignoring the woman lying beneath him, her
eyes turned to him in supplication. She was sobbing and
her abdomen joined in the protest with a good show of
blood. My cowardly toes were curling inside my shoes,
although the rest of me did nothing.

Removing the whole thick line of plastic did not take
long. When he was finished, Dr. Hanforth grabbed some
swabs and blotted them over the bleeding, sob-trembling
woman and nodded to me as if to say, you can take it
from here, at least? Surely? And he was off.

I cross the road and make for one of the side doors
into the hospital. My entrance is almost blocked by
square metal bins on huge wheels. Litter tumbles onto
the asphalt from their teeming summits. A graying
man in a tabard spikes bits of rubbish and puts
them back in the containers, pressing the bulk of the
garbage down to make room for what he is adding. I
walk past quickly.

I am almost sorry to discover that the seminar-room
door is open and that I am not going to be kept waiting this week. All the reading and preparation I did at
home has come to nothing pitted against this one short
trip to the hospital. I feel guilty and exhausted. I have
to remind myself of Julia, whom I left only a few hours

previously, of her love and her exhortation for me to keep calm. For me to be positive and not act as my own executioner.

Taking a deep breath, I hold my head high and walk into the room. I attempt to comfort myself with the thought that I am about to be confronted with a bog-standard psychiatrist, not some mystical soothsayer, but this lame attempt at bravura doesn't help. I resolve on calm but the truth is that there are all sorts of details which disconcert me. Not only that I didn't have a chance to collect myself in the waiting room, but other things. The chair I sat on before has been removed from the middle of the room and put against one of the walls. My new judge has drawn two seats slightly aside from the table and angled them towards each other. The window is open on a sky amok with clouds, and even the sound of midday traffic, rising up from the street where I was walking just a few moments earlier, sounds like a racket to me now.

Dr. Gilchrist comes forward and shakes my hand. He is lanky and quite old, but there is such steadiness in him. For a moment, I think I could feel strong again too, simply by being near him. This happens just before he pulls the rug from under my feet with his news. There is no change in my patient's condition: she is still unconscious and on assisted ventilation. By no means out of danger. I'm sure this was not meant as a weapon, this bald report, but I can hardly manage it. We are both standing, but he gestures to me to sit down, and I am glad to sink onto the chair. I can't mask my disappointment. My fate feels so linked to that of my patient. I'm not sure what the point of my defending myself will be if she dies. And

I know that the longer she spends in intensive care, the less likely she is ever to recover.

Maybe it is because I am thinking so intently of the woman I have harmed that I get off on the wrong foot with Dr. Gilchrist. I can't really remember the first few minutes of our conversation. Perhaps he asks me about my last week, about how I've been feeling. That sounds more or less right. Whatever has passed, I can't regain the lost ground. I would like to ask if we can begin again, but I know there's no point.

Everything I say to the psychiatrist, everything I fail to cope with in each second that elapses is more evidence against me. I'm sure he doesn't miss a trick. I try and gird myself. I can't afford to take my eye off the ball. I have to watch my manner at all times, give careful attention to the very modulation of my words, look my interrogator in the eye a reasonable amount: all of that. It's not easy, though. There's something about this man which provokes me, his sepia clothes, his wiry ankles, his bald determination to categorize me. The *Diagnostic and Statistical Manual of Mental Disorders* pokes from his hemp bag. I start listening intently and, suddenly, the psychiatrist's voice seems very loud.

"...if you had any doubts about whether you'd be able to handle it?"

"Sorry?"

"I'll repeat. Were you worried you wouldn't be able to handle it? I say, is my Scottish accent too much for you?"

"No, of course not. Handle *what?*"

"Medical school. Did you have any doubts—"

"No."

Have I caught his meaning? The nerve of him, I think.

If anyone has been too lame to rise to the challenges of hospital medicine, it isn't me. His papers are square on the desk in front of him and I can see neat handwriting at the top of the uppermost page. I don't remember him putting pen to paper. I wonder if he'll add to this report right now, or wait for me to leave the room before letting officious thoughts flow from his nib.

In place of the gray one in front of me, I imagine Julia's face. I try to soften my tone. "Well, actually, I'm not sure what you mean."

"In my life," he pauses to clear his throat, "I sometimes have an instinct that I should avoid something. I don't know, swimming in a rough sea, riding on the back of a motorbike, that kind of thing. When I ignore these instincts, it is usually at my peril."

The idea of him performing any of the stunts he describes strikes me as ridiculous. "No, I didn't have that feeling." I uncross my legs. I try to change the fix of my facial muscles. Perhaps relaxing my body will make me feel less combative.

"But you've had that sense before? You know what I'm talking about? If you had felt somewhere deep down that you were making the wrong decision, embarking on this career, you would have recognized it?"

"Why do you say that—'this career'? Seriously, why don't you say what you mean?"

He picks his pen up, spins it round once in his hand. "Is there something you think I'm leaving out?" He puts the pen down on the arm of his chair.

"Well, yes. My abortion work, obviously. That's what you're skirting around, isn't it? That's the thing you don't want to say out loud. A-bor-tion. Abortion." I am surprised at how strange and shocking the word sounds, even in my own mouth. I am not sure if I've ever said it before.

"And how do you feel, saying it out loud?"

"Oh, for goodness' sake! What is this? What are these questions? How does it feel to say it? Was I scared like a baby at medical school? That's what you were asking me before, isn't it? About my instincts. It's ridiculous. I mean, doctors' lives are full of disgusting things, full of events one's instinct, as you call it, rises up against. Dealing with the sick and dying. Performing horrible procedures on people. You know, spending two years cutting up dead people before tea isn't exactly genteel, is it? But we all do it. Even you must have done?"

He makes as if to talk, but I stop him. I lift up my hand.

"No. Let me tell you, the first time I touched our cadaver I was so spooked that I went home afterwards, put all my clothes in the wash, and scrubbed myself clean in the shower like bloody Meryl Streep in that movie. But, within a couple of weeks, I wasn't even bothering to wipe my hands after dissection. And you want to ask me about my instincts?"

My question hangs in the air. My aggression comes to nothing because Dr. Gilchrist doesn't retaliate. He's not interested in having a fight. He wants more from me than that. It would be easy to go quite limp in the circumstances, but I need to keep my wits about me. I feel deflated. After a minute, in which he writes, the psychiatrist looks up at me again. He smiles.

"I can see you're a plain-talker, Nancy. So. Why don't

you tell me this. What kind of person becomes an abortionist, do you think? What—"

"Abortion provider. Not an abortionist, an abortion provider."

"Ah. A provider, is it? Okay. Fair enough. Is there a type, though? Do you think there might be a type? Are you that type?"

I haven't come close to answering this question in my own mind yet, but I relax. I know what I can say. There's a rhetoric that goes with the job I do, and I'm familiar with it. I'm well versed enough in the matter to be able to provide an explanation. What other truth do I have? I put my hands in my lap and look at Dr. Gilchrist. I notice the arcus senilis in his eyes, which gives them a very slightly milky appearance.

"I think it does take a certain kind of person, yes. I mean, any surgery does. And I know we gynecologists aren't thought of as surgeons proper because operating isn't all we do. But we need the same qualities. To be determined, competitive, I suppose. Hard of stomach. Unsentimental. Yes. Because, however neutral you feel about the work—and there really is no reason not to feel neutral, is there? I mean, this is a legal procedure and women are entitled to it—however neutral you may feel, there are the sensibilities of others to be contended with. You know, people at work who may disagree with what you do. Doctors, nurses. And everyone outside work too—family, and so on. You have to be able to deal with all the baggage that everyone else brings to the table..."

I stare at Dr. Gilchrist's head as he writes his notes, remembering the first time I ever saw Frederick addressing my class of medical students, nearly a decade ago.

"It is safer to have an abortion in this country than it is to see a pregnancy to term" had been the first sentence of his lecture, dropped like a bomb. He must have witnessed the same herd reaction every time he delivered his lecture. First, a whole row of girls had moved, like one bashful invertebrate, along the bench and out of the lecture-room door. A few boys had joined them, grabbing the opportunity to play hooky. Quiet expectation had fallen upon those of us who remained. Frederick had opened a window and smiled, before beginning to teach us.

"So, it's more a question of dealing with other people's difficult feelings about your work than having to wrangle with your own?" Dr. Gilchrist is speaking again.

"Yes. Look, here's the thing. I consider it to be a life-saving procedure that I do, that we do. It's saving the life of a woman, it's something that saves a woman's freedom. And what is her life without this? It's painted in this bad light, but terminating a potential life is not the worst thing that can happen. What about finishing a woman's life before it's even started?"

My words sound thin to me. My thoughts feel full but not when I speak them aloud. They bleed out. Dr. Gilchrist clears his throat. He says, "I see." He attempts to clear his throat again. "Yes, that's a good, complete explanation." And I'm distracted. It reminds me of my dad, that noise. His eyes are red with the effort of getting his voice back. I'm not sure what I should do to help him. After a moment, Dr. Gilchrist, still struggling, excuses himself to get some water. He gestures his intention to me with his hands as he rises from his chair. I feel the air shift as he walks past me.

When he has gone, I listen to the traffic outside the window. I separate it into strands. A low-frequency sound posits itself as a van. I hear the noise, I know what it is. And there's another. A car, this time, surely? Why am I incapable of doing this with my own thoughts? Why can't I name them, bring them out, paint them truly? In my mind's eye I see myself standing next to Dr. Hanforth. Is that memory enough to make me bad? And now here I am extolling the virtues of toughness while at the same time a different scene entirely, that of a poor man lying in front of me in a hospital bed, reveals itself to me for the first time in years. Unravels into what I have been saying aloud, belies it. Experiences rise up to defend as well as accuse me. It is as if my patients stand in the wings, each of them leaning on one or the other side of the argument. How on earth am I to begin to understand what has happened, let alone how much I have been to blame, when it seems that everything that can be said about me is both true and also not true? I am a brute and I have the evidence. But I am compassionate too.

It must have been someone's birthday. That's what I thought when I walked in that morning because there was a joyful hubbub, a humorous sound lightening the everyday train-station noises of the ward. A few nurses were gathered together near the central station, the one made from the long desk and the couple of computers and the trolley of patient notes. And the nurses weren't huddled over something so much as leaning on each others' shoulders to support themselves. They were catching their breath between bouts of laughter.

I drew closer and I saw my colleague, Matt, an intern

just like me and a real hit with the nurses. He had the right body. He looked as if he'd sailed on well-built boats in clement bays. His jaw was square, his eyes bovine. He was good-natured too. He was standing there, anyway, in his clean white coat, arms crossed over his handsome chest, looking benignly at the nurses, indulging their joke, whatever it was. I saw how his tolerant stance encouraged this gaggle to new levels of mirth and how each of these women felt the possibility that the handsome young doctor's regard might fall on them. I watched them find singular ways to look amused and pretty for him.

There was a West Indian nurse leading the fun, keeping the joke alive. Every time she straightened up and wiped tears from her eyes to offer another jest, the others paused with her, readying themselves for another short lease of laughter to do their best with, to shape to their own sexy advantage. I marveled at this nurse, at the ease with which she could create such a festive scene.

"Now when you finish here, Matt, you just come along with me to *my* house. I find *plenty* for you to do about the place with that there apron on!" she said, enjoying the lengthened drama of her own Caribbean vowels, which prompted new peals of laughter all around.

Matt came forward to me. The thin plastic apron tied around his slim waist shone along the length of him. He touched me and it was as if this made me visible: for a second or two, I felt the great bounty of being drawn into the group on whose periphery I had been standing, invisible. But it was short-lived, this pleasure. It stopped ever so quickly. The nurses, having spotted me, started to collect themselves. They were still smiling and murmuring but they did not exactly bother to hide the fact that my appearance on the scene had soured their game.

Matt didn't pick up on this slight change of mood, and his continuing jocularity kept a couple of nurses close by as he said to me, rather loudly in fact, "I've been asked to learn a new skill, Nancy, and perform manual evacuation of feces on a patient." There was a single squeal from one of the more dogged sisters. "Apparently, none of our nursing colleagues has been on the course that teaches this skill. I, of course, pointed out that neither you nor I have, or ever will go on that course. But Mary informs me that, since we're doctors, it's fine for us to just hop in and give it a go. She's not going to do it herself, but she's kindly offered to stand by and supervise."

"And now that Nancy has turned up, you can do it together." All the others dispersed, leaving the pert young Mary in charge of the situation. I was afraid of her. She had short bleached hair and her attitude was poised between the affection she was sending out to Matt and the hostility she wanted to make quite plain to me. "Better get an apron and some gloves. Your man's right there," she said, pointing her chin to the cubicle next to us, not bothering to unfold her arms from under the ledge of her pretty bust. "Bed three."

I went into the stocks room to get the things we would need, and when I came back I saw, from the empty space beside the nurses' table and the drawn curtain around bed three, that Mary and Matt had gone ahead of me. I felt a pulse of shame on seeing how near the patient was all along to where the nurses had been laughing just a few minutes before, although it was also from the feeling of being left out. It seemed as if Mary could read my mind, for when I joined my colleagues behind the curtain she said to me, "Don't worry yourself, Nancy, he's not really with it, this one."

I looked down at the bed. It was easier to look at a sick patient than at Matt and Mary. It was easier to look at a back curved with pain. I tried to ascertain what was wrong with the man lying in the bed, as this gave me a good, public reason to be resting my eyes on him. What illness might he have which would require the performance of an act I had never heard of before then? His sheets had been pulled back. He was positioned on one side, facing the window, his back exposed to the three of us. His pajamas had been pulled down, his knees hitched up. Mary must have done this too. I noticed how flat and wasted the muscles on his bottom were and, just as Matt began to speak, I observed the suction dressing stuck to a large area of his sacrum.

"He's got some neuro condition. Mother tries to look after him at home, but he's got shocking sores so he's here for what the tissue viability nurse can do. Then probably on to a care home."

I wondered about our patient's level of awareness. As an ignorant intern, I knew it wouldn't help me to hear the name of the neurological condition this man was suffering from but, with nothing more than eyes in my head, I could see that the man curled up and half naked on the bed in front of us was conscious. I didn't understand why no one was talking to him, explaining what we were doing, something I'd seen nurses make a point of, even with babies in their care. I couldn't understand why no one else was concerned about how it might seem to him, to hear a group of nurses and a doctor laughing right outside his cubicle over the sheer comedy of who was going to have the horrible job of looking after his needs.

Matt squirted a transparent worm of K-Y Jelly onto his gloved hand, found the patient's anus and inserted two fingers. Seconds later, he dropped a few small, dark pellets into the kidney dish Mary was holding next to our patient's buttocks on the bed, and she said, "Bingo!"

On his second try, Matt came back with nothing. I noticed how close Mary's face moved to his when he leaned in, because of how she was holding the bowl in place and, on his third attempt, she smiled directly at him and challenged him, "Go on, Matt, go a bit deeper." I heard the patient groan but this time Matt pulled his hand straight out and, surprising Mary and myself, said to me, "Mate, I can't do this. I just can't. I swear I'm gonna bloody puke if I carry on." And so Mary, miffed that he had chosen me and not her to address in this moment of crisis, took her gloves off and said, "You'd better see what you can do then, Nancy."

Matt stood up next to me in the small cubicle. Because of his height, his hands came nearer my face than I would have liked. "I'm really sorry, Nancy. Do you mind?" he asked. "I owe you one." I could smell the feces on his gloves. All I wanted was for him to leave, for I knew Mary would leave then too. By myself, I would be able to try my hardest to rise to the occasion. So, I said, "Really, it's no problem. I'll page you when I'm finished and we'll go through the other jobs."

Mary and Matt left and I remained there feeling lily-livered. I stood at the bedside of my patient and didn't know how to rally. I berated myself for allowing sympathy to obstruct me, for letting emotion get in the way of the job that needed to be done. I resolved that I would not find myself wanting, as Matt had just done.

So, as I squirted jelly onto my own index and middle finger and smoothed it over the rest of my hand, I did not let myself look again at what I could see of my patient's face, but fixed my eyes on the window in front of me. As I held one buttock out of the way, I noticed that this window gave onto a dark brick wall a few feet beyond the glass. Putting my fingers into the man on the bed, I concentrated on the pattern of these bricks, three laid horizontally next to three laid vertically, next to three laid horizontally. Feeling my hand curl around solid excrement, I actively ignored the sounds I heard from the bed and willed myself not to think about the body beneath me, moving away from my digital search, concluding instead that it must be a gray day outside from the lightless color of the bricks on the wall.

But, as I brought out a mass of feces into the bowl, my momentary trance failed me and I retched, tasting stomach acid in my mouth, only just managing not to vomit. And with this, I saw everything as it was. I could see distress in my patient's profile, could hear that the noises he made were noises of pain and resistance, and I felt that old familiar feeling of shame, the strong emotion that had been my enemy in the general surgery clinic and now threatened to sabotage me again.

I knew my job was far from done, and was galvanizing myself to try again, to detach myself, when my eyes happened upon my patient's bedside table. On it was the hospital phone, the regulation hospital tissues, a maroon flannel in a blue dish. But just behind this I saw something that interested me more. It was an old-fashioned hairbrush, like my granny used to have. Silver-backed and with an ornate silver handle and pale, almost uselessly soft bristles. The ones that usually come in a set with a looking glass and a comb. And on this hairbrush I could just make out three initials, barely visible in its worn and shiny surface.

Reflexively, because I had been reminded of my dead granny, my eyes cast about for something to confirm this memory, to stop it from fading as quickly as it had arisen before I had caught proper hold of it, and my eyes fell back on my patient. His hands were drawn up to his face. Perhaps, had I not been thinking about my granny, I might not have made the connection that my patient was about the same age as my dad. But I did, and I felt sad to see a man of that age with his hands at his face like a child. And the weight in my mind of the hairbrush and the hands and my dead granny and dad was such that I rested my left hand on my patient's back for relief. As I did this, I felt him relax. Then, without making a decision, but just naturally, I went about my work. With five or six passes I managed to clear my patient's rectum. I felt I was gentle and efficient, and I was glad to do it because I knew my patient wasn't scared anymore and neither was I. And I looked at that damn wonderful hairbrush and thanked it in my head for making me realize something important that had been beyond me until that time. That it would never work for me to disengage from my patients. That I would only be able to do the horrible things my job would require by doing the exact opposite. Standing by that man's bed, with shit on my hands and a bowl full of shit in front of me, I knew that I would never forget what I had learned. And that no patient of mine would ever again feel they had been treated like meat in my care.

I look up to find Dr. Gilchrist sitting in front of me. The angle of the light in the room has changed, altering my interrogator's appearance. He sits absolutely still, and all the folds and creases and cuffs of his clothes appear as different shades of green and brown and blue. Woodland hues, not gray at all. I wonder how long he's been there, for how many minutes I've been daydreaming right in front of him. There are two glasses of water newly placed on the table in between us and I watch the meniscus on each tremble. When the psychiatrist speaks, his voice is different.

"I didn't set out to be a psychiatrist, you know, Nancy. Not at all. I went to medical school with the same grand visions of myself, of what I might amount to in the future, as anyone. But those grand visions didn't last long in my case. They only got me as far as the emergency department. I was working in a hospital near Glasgow at the time, still living with my parents. I'd been in the job maybe a day or two, and I was doing just fine. And then a trauma alert came in one evening. A knife fight. They were bringing in a whole bunch of lads who'd been at each other, ten or twelve of them. The boss-man said there'd be lots of sewing to do, anyone who could throw a suture should get ready. Just the ticket, I thought.

"Suddenly, the department was full of shouting and blood. The boys the crew dragged in were injured, but they were still at each other. Blood was literally flying around. Their faces were gashed and there were bloody

T-shirts and then this young lad was carried past me. He wasn't fighting because he was in a bad way. He was on a gurney, being taken into the trauma bay, and there was a bobby walking next to the paramedic, carrying a machete. And I tell you, for a moment, I thought it was the most ghastly thing I'd ever seen until I looked down on the stretcher and saw that the man lying on it had only one of his arms. The other one wasn't attached to him anymore. It was kind of laid alongside him, but not connected to him, if you know what I mean. And that was the last thing I knew, before I hit the deck. I don't know how long I lay there for. I guess everyone was too busy to pick me up. But eventually I came to. I was all covered in blood from the floor. And I almost wished I didn't have to get up because of the shame. Everything around me was business-as-usual. I went and got changed. I carried on for the rest of the shift and, you know, no one said a thing. But there was no coming back from that. So I've always wondered. What did I lack? What makes you lot, who are okay with all that blood, different to me? Did you have a moment, an equal and opposite moment from the one I had, when you saw claret for the first time, maybe, and you thought, Wow, look at all this blood and guts. I can really do this?"

Red autumn. Second year as a doctor. Outside my home there is leaf-smell, and the air sparkles clearer than water. I am at my desk. My window is open and I have been sitting there for hours reading an endocrinology book, because a woman has been admitted to my ward with a rare hormone disease called acromegaly, and I want to learn all about it before I meet her. But I am about to completely stop thinking about medicine. The phone rings. It is Julia, and she speaks directly to my heart. Tom, is what she says. This is all I hear. Tom. He's back. My sister talks slowly to me and then she stays quietly on the end of the phone. She knows full well that no one has dethroned him. I listen to her breathing. When I'm ready, she hangs up. I look back at the colorful text in front of me, but its pages hold no drama now. I close the book and stand up. I lean right out of the window and, stretching my face up to the sky, I breathe. The air is rich with leaves, and the leaves by my window are herald colors. The pavements are laden with brightness and I gaze all the way along these avenues of red and orange and yellow.

I look hard at the glass of water Dr. Gilchrist has brought me, focus on the distinctness of the vessel, the purity of its contents. I try to keep its outline very clear. I pick it up just to feel it in my hand, the verifiable truth of it. I take a sip. What good are all these thoughts if they stay in my head? I know I need to speak. No one else is going to defend me. It's up to me to represent myself, to describe myself as I wish to be understood. When my voice does come, I am reassured by how I sound. "She was my first surgical patient and her name was Violet." The words select themselves. And with this one sentence, the story I am happy to tell asserts itself over the one I cannot.

"I was in my second year of training when I met Violet. I was working for a team of endocrinologists at the time, and I just loved the job. There's that perfect logic about the pathophysiology of hormone diseases and, when I wasn't on the ward, I was in the library. All my bosses were so brainy."

My knee almost touches Dr. Gilchrist's. We are much closer together than we were, and both leaning forward on our seats. It feels nice to have his full attention, to know where I am heading, to be putting one foot steadily in front of the other.

"She came into hospital on a Friday. One of the fellows gave me the tip-off. He knew it would only be a matter of time before every medical student and intern in the establishment would be hanging around her, wanting to check her out. He advised me to get in there before the weekend. But I didn't go and see her that day. I didn't want to treat her like some kind of freak show. I wanted to learn about her disease before I approached her. So I took a book out of the library. It was a beautiful autumn and I remember poring over that book at home, at a table by the window, for hours that weekend. The following week, though, I pretty much took up residence by her bedside."

"She was that interesting?"

"She was. And she was a welcome focus."

"Because?"

"She just was. Look, I don't want to get off track. What was I saying? I went in on the Monday, keen as mustard, really impatient to meet her. I'd made myself wait. I'd studied pretty much everything there was to know about her illness. And I wondered if I'd recognize her, from all that I'd learned. Would I know her across a room? Would my instincts lead me to her?

"I walked onto the ward—and it was just as I'd hoped

it would be. I knew exactly who she was as soon as I clapped eyes on her. She was in the middle bay, in the bed nearest the walkway. Unlike everyone else on the ward, however, folded into blankets, twisted this way and that or hidden behind curtains, she was sitting in her chair, knitting.

"She had the characteristic mighty big skull and big bony ridges over her eyes because of the tumor in her brain producing too much growth hormone, but her hair was soft and silvery and feminine as anything. Her nose was huge and so were her ears and lips, but the dressing gown she wore looked like it might be a Liberty print. Her forearms were graceful and she wore a gold lady's watch but this only emphasized her hands. They were like butcher's hands, massive, with thick meaty fingers. She was like a bizarre mixture of total femininity and monstrousness. I remember thinking, here is a woman who has literally outgrown herself, who doesn't fit her own skin anymore."

"Then what?"

"She beckoned me over. She must have noticed me standing there, textbook in hand, staring. It might have offended someone else, but not Violet. She welcomed me from the outset. When I went over to her she took my hand and introduced herself to me. It was the opposite of the usual order of things. I sat down on her bed and that was the beginning of what I really would like to call a friendship. But I know that doesn't sound right, so how's this? That was the beginning of me and Violet. The start of how important she became to me. I mattered to her, too. Even now, I still believe that."

I have another drink. It gives me an opportunity to

look again at Dr. Gilchrist. It's good to see the expression on his face, to mark the effect that my words can have.

"I was busy, of course. Every day was hectic. In the mornings I'd rush about on the ward round, getting whatever my seniors needed, making long lists of tasks. Afterwards, it could take me hours to get all these jobs done. But when I completed my work each day, I went to Violet. She was like a reward, a comfort or something. We liked to sit together with her notes and have a look at any new results, track the ebb and flow of her electrolytes. She was particularly interested in the circular photos taken by the colonoscope, which showed the folds of her bowel. I remember Violet saying she thought they looked like petals, all heaped up on some curious plant.

"But it wasn't always clinical conversations we had. She told me plenty of other stuff about herself as well. I heard about her antiques business, about her husband who'd died a few years before. Even about a girl called Kitty, who she remembered from her childhood. And there were other things too, you know, funny things. She had a basket she'd hung from her kitchen ceiling, which she kicked every morning, to reassure herself she was still fit. She even kept a shotgun under her bed.

"Anyway, one afternoon, maybe a couple of weeks after we met, I was sitting in my usual spot with Violet. For once we weren't talking. Violet was knitting and I was just sitting beside her. A doctor I'd never seen before turned up. He wasn't part of my team. I thought he must have got the wrong bed at first, but it was Violet he was after, all right. He was Dr. O'Keefe, he said, and he was a surgeon. He'd come to discuss the operation he would be performing to remove Violet's pituitary tumor. Just like that. I don't think anyone had mentioned the possibility of surgery to her before. And he just blundered in and said he'd be cutting her open later that week.

"She was really shocked, I could tell. There had been some discussion about the different treatments that were available, but surgery had never seemed to be top of the list. We'd certainly not discussed it, she and I. And suddenly, here was this guy, who might as well have had a knife in his hand right there and then. I could see he had no idea—no conception at all of how she was feeling. Of what it might mean to a person to have to consider being put under anesthetic, to think about completely losing control like that, to have something done to her that would change her forever. An operation she would never be able to undo—"

"But, Nancy, she was ill. She had a tumor. Wasn't he just trying to help her, this surgeon?"

"Yes. Yes, of course he was. But he really did not consider her feelings at all."

"Okay. So, then what?"

"I didn't know what she was going to do. I reckon I was more upset than she was, hearing the details of how he was going to remove her tumor. But then she surprised both of us. She gave a little speech which, truly, I'll never forget. First, she introduced me to the specialist. You should have seen his face! She said how much I'd comforted her during her stay in hospital. She referred to me as her lucky charm. And the long and short of it was she agreed to go ahead with the op but only on condition that I was there, next to her, through all of it. I don't know who must have looked more horrified. Me, because I'd never been at all keen on going to theater, or him for having this hopeless young doctor foisted on him by one of his patients. But one thing was clear: neither of us had much of a choice in the matter."

"So, what happened then? What was it like in theater?"

Dr. Gilchrist sounds so keen, so boyish almost, that for a second I think he must be mocking me. Yet it's clear he's completely genuine. He's beaming. It's the first time I've seen him smile.

"I wanted to see Violet before she was put under anesthetic, so I got up especially early on the day of her operation. I felt queasy, but I made myself eat a banana."

"You'd heard enough about what happened to rookies who couldn't deal with the sight of blood to know you should take precautions."

"I was still feeling a bit sick on the bus—"

"Nerves?"

"—so I reviewed the whole course of my relationship with Violet in my head, played it over, from the time we'd met. I thought about how stoical she'd been, and started to feel bad about how little I'd considered this before, how awful it must have been for her, while I was just enjoying her company. I suppose I felt a bit ashamed of how selfish I'd been because I started thinking, for the first time, that the surgery was in fact a really good thing after all, even though I didn't like the guy who was going to do it, because it would make Violet better and she'd be able to get home at last."

"And you were trying to settle your nerves too, am I right?"

"Maybe I was. Quite possibly. Although it was really

Violet who ended up doing that for me as well. So, I got to the hospital, went to the ward, determined to cheer Violet up. She was all ready. Even the way she was lying on her bed, stiff as a board, was like she was showing her readiness to be operated on. And, of course, she wasn't a bit scared, didn't need any reassurance from me. There I was, ready to cajole her, and there was no need. I was—"

"—all revved up with no place to go."

"Worse than that. I realized how well she'd got to know me because, despite my cheery-cheery look, she could tell I was feeling rotten and—"

"—she comforted you?"

"Yes. But in a strict kind of way. 'Stop hiding yourself under a stone, Nancy.' That was exactly what she said. She wanted me to push myself forward more, I think. She even told me to enjoy myself. In theater, I mean."

"And did you?"

"To begin with, when I left her and went to put scrubs on, I think I was putting a brave face on for Violet's sake. Because she had been so brave, and I knew she wanted me to be more positive."

"And, when you got into theater?"

"Things changed. You know it, don't you? You can tell from my—"

"—from what I remember myself. So, what—"

"I walked over the threshold. And I felt it instantly, the excitement. I was amazed by it. But only for a second before Violet was wheeled in, under anesthetic, and I reminded myself it was her I was there for. Two guys moved her to the center of the room and lifted her onto the operating table. I saw a single strand of Violet's hair billowing as they lifted her across. In no time, her entire body was covered in drapes, sheets of green paper. You could see where the folds had been, and the paper was tented over prominences, over her knees and stomach and her face. One minute, she was there in front of me and then she wasn't. It was like a shroud."

"And how did you feel, seeing her like that? Did you feel bad?"

"No. It just reminded me of my childhood. My sister and I built a miniature landscape once with forests and a lake made from foil, and a quarry made with gravel from the street. I stared at Violet's sheathed body without focusing, imagining its contours to be those others. Then suddenly Dr. O'Keefe was standing there and I remember the weird tilting, having to readjust my perspective."

"Did he acknowledge you?"

"More. He said, 'Are you going to scrub, or what?' "

"Wow."

"I know. I was so grateful to Violet, for the conversation that morning, for the way she'd encouraged me. Now my nerves were long gone. My pulse was through the ceiling but it wasn't fear anymore, it was excitement, and I was glad I didn't have to feel bad about that, or guilty. I was the first assistant, you know—there was no one else. I was essential to the surgery Violet needed. If the anesthesiologist had held her stethoscope to my chest she would have heard it going like the clappers.

"A nurse helped me to scrub. It took me a while to get the hang of it. And when I went back into theater what I beheld was a wonderland. With a space in it for me. I went over to the table, my gloved hands over my chest like the nurse had shown me. The room scintillated around us, the grand specialist, Violet in her landscape of green, and me. The floor was buffed and gleaming. Three or four OR techs, looking just like surgeons apart from the different color of their caps, busied themselves quietly around the room. The anesthesiologist sat enthroned in her machines.

"And—maybe I can only say this to another doctor—but it was a perfect universe, all action, no need for talking. A place with no rough or imperfect surfaces. No windows to remind you of the real world outside. The only view was into the operating theater next to ours, through a small window. In there, I could see another surgical team bending over their work.

"When Dr. O'Keefe took the scope from the nurse, my heart was beating like a hammer. My fingers prickled. 'Freer,' he said and I was thrilled by his code. I loved the fact that a syllable foreign to me could refer to the instrument she passed him. It was like a slim metal handle slightly flattened and curved at one end.

"When the scope went into Violet's nostril, the black screen flared into a perfect red circle showing the inside of her nose. Then Dr. O'Keefe handed the scope to the nurse for a moment and took my hands in his own. He placed them on the sterile drapes in front of me so that I wouldn't make the mistake of dropping them to my sides and needing to rescrub. I felt his hands on mine, their great weightiness and then the lightness when they were gone. He started operating and he explained everything that he was doing, softly, because he was concentrating.

"And I knew Violet wouldn't mind what I was thinking—which was that it was much better than being on the wards. It felt incredible to be a part of this procedure, to be actually assisting in it. On the screen, I saw Dr. O'Keefe pressing a pink structure inside the nose over to one side, where it seemed to stick, before he went further. Then he went through the choana, at the end of the nostril, and found the sphenoid ostium. He pushed into it, then pressed forwards. He called it tiger country. He had to go through the back of the sinus, right next to the optic nerves, the cavernous sinuses. It was astonishing. He was so calm. Next thing I knew, he'd made this hole—I could see it on the screen—and he was cutting through the dura, and he found what he wanted: the tumor. There it was, for the taking. On the screen it looked huge. And nothing could stop him now, this man, he was hooking the tumor out through Violet's nostril. When he put the scope back in, all that appeared on the screen was blood and I was afraid. But then he inserted an instrument into her and everything was brought under his control. Lakes of red disappeared into the metal rod and against the lateral wall of the nose I could see quite clearly where the blood was coming from. Dr. O'Keefe directed his sucker there, so that the red went straight into the gray with none escaping, and then there was a single prolonged beep as he controlled the diathermy on the instrument and cauterized the bleeding vessel. As smoke curled out of Violet's nose I realized that this was what I was seeing on the screen, only magnified, so that it appeared like a sandstorm, like a cloud of sparkling confetti."

My story is suddenly over. I have reached the conclusion of the series of events I embarked on telling. But I don't feel finished. It's as if I've just warmed up, should still be in the middle of things. I watch Dr. Gilchrist scribble away on his pad. I wonder if he senses that I haven't finished, if he will help me find a way to start again. He stops writing. His smile is not an opening but a gesture of punctuation. He puts his pen down, turns to look out of the window where we both see clearly that the sky has darkened. He looks at his watch. I do not like these signs.

"We're very nearly done, Nancy. I just have a few quick questions for you before I let you go. Starting with this. In the weeks leading up to your crisis in theater, did you have any avoidant or intrusive symptoms? I'm sorry, it's awkward talking to colleagues, isn't it? Did you feel, for example, less sociable than usual? Did you want to hide yourself away during this time?"

"I'm a private type of person." I have always been. But now I want to talk.

"More so recently?"

"Leading up to that day. Perhaps."

"And were you extra tired, finding it hard to concentrate, longing to be by yourself?"

"The doctor's condition?" Can I question him back into letting me speak?

"Perhaps. And have there been—were there any unusual dreams? Flashbacks to...?"

"To?"

"To your abortion work."

There it is again. This axe of a word. This bomb, cutlass, guillotine. He has to twist his mouth to say it. He wants nothing to do with his own lips and tongue, for contriving to be so obscene. I know this. But I want to start saying the things I never have before. I can't believe I have missed this chance. I have told a half story to this man, when I could have—

"Any dreams?"

"Yes, you do get dreams. I have had them, I mean. Maybe a few times a week, before. Dead baby dreams. They're up in trees. They stare at me with yellow eyes. Or carpets of babies' backs. Or dreams where just one baby looks at me, but its anger is like that of a grown-up."

"Okay, I get it."

We face each other full on and silently. The only power I have left is the power to shock. His voice comes to me softly now, not asking for so much.

"Still? Since you've stopped working?"

"No. Nothing since that day in theater."

No one likes this kind of talk. Not even a psychiatrist, who must have heard all sorts. In any case, he has probably arrived at his destination, his conclusion as to how to name my mental state. Burnout? I wonder. Or something like it. And I have misused my time. Although I have put some things that actually happened in order and have reported these events accurately, I see that this isn't enough. The psychiatrist is waiting. He is rising to shake my hand, to encourage me to rise too. He is impatient to marry his thoughts to one of the long list of psychiatric diagnoses in his *DSM-IV*. Before he excuses me, he has a final question, but I sense my answer won't make a difference.

"Becoming a gynecologist. You just liked the work? Or was it anything in particular?"

I pause for a moment before giving an answer commensurate with all the others I have offered during this hour-long session.

"Nothing in particular, no."

How long does it take before the other story begins to unfurl? I don't think I have even left the room. Maybe it is when I cross the threshold from the carpeted area, in which Dr. Gilchrist and I have conferred, to the linoleum of the hospital where sounds replace silence. The two floors are part of the same hospital just as my two tales are part of the same few weeks of my life. Is this what it is to be a woman, this divorcing from its untidy twin a neat version fit for public consumption? The version we can live with from the one that unhinges us? It is enough that I am not aware of my journey home, or of walking through the building that I love into the angry streets which harbor it. That my bus trip passes like a dream. That I don't know how I get from the bus stop to my flat. What I remember takes me all the way back to my desk where I find I have thrown my window open again and am looking back out on the trees, now bare, where this recollection began.

The other story. The B-side. The background against which my relationship with Violet glows so brightly. The drama in which my dear Violet must take a bow, white hair billowing, in which she must graciously hand over her script, in which she must accede to being only a player in the drama of the life of Nancy, where she must become a bit part, where the main role is to be played by someone called Tom.

Julia tells me about a party. Tons of the old crowd will be there. It is a fairy tale, it is the setting in which we will be reunited. Such events have enacted themselves since the beginning of history. I start to think about my appearance for the first time in years. Cinderella in rags, covered in dust but so pretty underneath it, brushing her ashes away, longing for the ball, birds swooping to help her pick up the peas, peck, peck, peck. She must have dreamed too of the finery she would wear to the ball to meet the love who would know her instantly. I don't own any makeup. I don't know what fashion is, but what does that matter? There is surely enough beauty in finding the person you have lost.

I go there. I'm not a single bit bothered that I don't know anyone. I am a virtuoso at being invisible. I am in trousers and trainers. I am quite different from all the others. I am surely not unlike that girl of ten years ago. I am still strong and brave. I am all the things that made him love me. There are people everywhere. They move from room to room. They garland the stairs. A guy I've never met hands me a beer and starts to talk to me. He runs through long lists of people he knows, certain we will find someone in common. There is only one person in my canon. His name is a scar in my head. I stand my ground. I am satisfied with my watch point. I look, from the corner of my eye, for Tom's blond head.

After an hour, I move to the first floor and I see him. He is talking to a group of girls. They are a different species to me. They gleam with sequins; their faces are like sunsets. I look at the man who is looking at me for a few seconds before I realize it is Tom because, of course, he has changed. He is not blond anymore. He is thin now. He is surrounded by girls. I wait for what is meant to happen, for the crowd to part, for Tom to approach me. In an instant this becomes the version that is only in my head. The real situation is different. Tom raises a hand to me in greeting. His hand is at half-mast. Then, I see his back again. I am examining it. What muscles are there? Rotator cuff, rhomboids, latissimus dorsi, deltoid. I receive no encouragement: nothing comes to me. This is what I have come all this way for. Not just to this party, you understand, but all the way through my life. And, in fairness, my heart does sink.

The party thins out. I move up a floor and down a floor. Everyone except me is drunk. I am much more wretched than that. I am disappointed. I am crushed that this hasn't amounted to more. I am actually bereft. When Tom does approach me, eventually, tapping me on the shoulder so that I have to swing around to him, I see that he is drunk too, and hear it in his voice. It is quite natural, I suppose, that he wants to tell me about the last ten years of his life. He has been to university. He has started a trekking company. He has recently climbed Kilimanjaro. He is not the boy he was. But my new impressions are as insubstantial as cobwebs compared to the hours and years of dreaming banked up against my memory of him. He is impressed, in a brittle way, that I have become a doctor. I hope he'll remember something about the way I was as a child that led me to this point, but he doesn't seem to. I hope he'll say anything at all about the time we spent together as kids, so I can see light shining in his face again, so that we can talk about that time as I have been unable to these past ten years with anyone.

Bathed in nostalgia as I am, it takes me some time to realize that Tom is going about the humdrum business of seducing me. I've dreamed of this, but not so emptily. I want to pour significance into what is happening. I want to give our conversation the shape and smell of the Blue Ridge Mountains. But I am eclipsed by the momentum of routine. And I don't want to miss out on what is afoot, however paltry it may be.

At the top of the house, there is a room with coats on the bed and a bolt on the door. Tom's adult face is soon above mine. But it is his fourteen-year-old face I choose to see, in those Virginia mountains. His hand held out to me offers me something outside of myself, seems to promise me the chance of being a different sort of girl than the one I am becoming. I jump over to him, feel both wild and safe. And in that dingy adult room, I do not get off the bed to find my bag. I do not stop for a conversation. I do not pause to find the condoms I have carried everywhere with me since the first time I had sex. I barely move. I lie beneath Tom and, though I am having sex, sex is not a fraction of what I want. I keep very still because, the truth is, I can't believe my luck. If I move an inch, say a word, my dream of ten years might end. I might break the spell. I might make myself concrete and unfriendly precisely when I want this man, above all else, to find me beautiful.

The party slams shut. It doesn't flower into the night. Sex does not buy me the opportunity to sleep with the man I have loved for years. He leaves the room, and the house, without me. And then come the days in which I have to learn to live with this feeling of slamming shut, repeating itself over and over. Of slamming, and then things being quite shut. Sometimes, I wake in the middle of the night, grateful that I belong to a hospital whose lights are never extinguished. Sometimes, I get up and shower as early as four in the morning. Or sometimes it is five, more civilized and less crazy, if my radio is whispering farming nuggets to me rather than the spaceless World Service. And then I put on something smart enough to wear on the wards but practical enough to cycle in. And I let myself out of the flat, helmet and bicycle clips already on. I march along the path to where my bike is parked just outside, holding its lights already lit, one a white glare, the other strobing redly. And during silent pedaling, the day arrives like a watercolor as I cycle so that by the time I arrive at the hospital the sky is not quite black but bluish at the edges: the concrete morning is nearly here, I have got to at least the threshold of another day.

And, in these mornings after Tom, there is Violet who is always pleased to see me when I approach her through the dark of the ward, where the nighttime smells of those sleeping around her still cluster, not yet blown through by the doors that will soon be opening and closing to bring ward rounds, groups of doctors who will swirl this air away, replacing it with their own scent of showers and adrenaline.

After a few weeks, I discover I am pregnant.

As I wait out the long days between one panel session and another, I continue to make early morning visits to the hospital. I suppose it is a sort of superstition that drives me. I hope that my intense sitting will make some sort of difference to my patient, the woman I have been prohibited from looking after in my usual, more rational way.

Although I move slightly further away from the Intensive Care Unit with each of these visits—I don't want to be noticed—wherever I choose to sit, I notice lowly workers striving in the gloaming. Housekeepers, their job titles branded in white letters on their uniform sweatshirts, are summoned to situations that nurses will no longer involve themselves in. They saunter to wherever blood or shit or ascites or anything else disgusting has been spilled, excreted or expelled. Orderlies push patients around this miniature city from one test or probing to another, and back to the wards again. And security guards, with big arms and hangdog faces, lope towards knots of strife on this ward or that.

I start to recognize people who work on the unit. I see the same nurses come and go although none recognize me in my civvies. There is a doctor though, who does. He has a red-and-white motorcycle helmet and his boots are always dirty. He looks a bit familiar to me in that way that many doctors do when you have worked the London hospitals for a few years. Sometimes he says hi to me as he passes. I am always too busy wondering about my patient to stop to work out where I've seen him before.

Then, one morning, just when I think he is about to pass by, he sits down suddenly beside me on the short bank of molded hospital chairs. He is huge next to me and, with some irritation, I am unable to keep my thoughts steady with him so near. I had been imagining what my patient's blood pressure might be, her respiratory rate, other markers of her physiological state, but now my mind is forced into an unwelcome state of expectation.

To add insult to injury, the doctor does not speak

straightaway; he just fidgets. It is the closest I have been to anyone in a while, and he is the most obtrusive person I have been near for ages. He drums his feet. He clenches and unclenches his fingers, so that I am aware of each and every one of them. He knots his hands together and then lets them fall to his sides, very close to my body. He undoes a button on his white coat and does it up again. He runs his hand through his hair, forcing me to notice the very bounce of it. What finally comes out of his mouth seems casual, indolent even, compared to the frenetic activity of his body. "Long shifts you're doing here on sentry duty. Surgery?"

I am surprised by his voice, which is deeper than I expected. And by his East Coast American accent. I am also surprised by myself for sounding almost normal.

"Ob-gyn." I put my hand inside my cardigan, ready to pull out my ID badge if the doctor becomes troublesome. Having exchanged a comment with him, I am now aware of more than his limbs. Big face, wide mouth, heavy eyebrows. Not pretty, but handsome. Hence the imposing nature, no doubt.

"Right. But you're considering defecting. You figure, after all those hours going crazy on the labor ward, you'd rather come and join us on the unit?"

I am not sure how to extricate myself. I shouldn't be here. I wonder if he might tell me something about my patient. Again I am struck by something familiar about him.

"I've a patient with you. But I can't come in and see her." I gesture at my clothes as if this might explain my situation. It would have been better to leave, but I can't resist the possibility that I might get some information if

I stay. I might have to be a little less hostile if I'm to get anything out of him. I turn to him properly for the first time.

"You're from the States."

"Ah..." He looks pleased. "My mom's English. She was worried about raising us there. Thought we might turn out too...how do you say it? Squeaky-clean?"

There is another long pause. The doctor is thinking about his past but I don't want to know about him. I sit very still until he speaks again. I am relieved when he starts to tell me about the only person who matters to me right now.

"Okay, so, our gyn patient. Corner bed. Let me see..." He rests his fingers together. He faces me and shuts his eyes. Trusting. Handsome. As I scrutinize him, he looks directly at me.

"But does that make you the doctor who...? The doctor?"

I wish I could disappear. "Yes. Me. Which is why..." I look down at my clothes again. I really want to leave now, but he was just about to tell me something. I'm sure of it. I should have stayed away. My heart starts to beat too fast. I pick up my bag, but then stop because I feel the man's hand on my arm. I am amazed by the weight of it. I am stilled by it completely.

"No, please don't scurry off." He smiles with that broad mouth of his. "Hey, I'm David, and I've fucked up multiple times." He raises a hand. We used to pledge allegiance like that at school in America. "Look, your patient is stable. At least, she was last night. We're looking after her."

"But how is she actually doing? I want details. I mean,

all I can do is wonder and wonder. And, if only I knew a bit more, I—"

"You could what? Sit here freaking out even more? Wouldn't you be better off doing something else? It's not like she's on her own."

Seconds pass but the doctor doesn't say anymore. He has found me out. He's disturbed my concentration but that's all. Suddenly I feel hopeless.

"Okay, so you're obviously not going to tell me anything. Why are you still sitting here, then? I mean, what's the point in sitting here if you have nothing to say?"

"Well, you know, it really isn't that I haven't got anything to say," he tells me. "A person can just sit quietly."

I've had enough, though. I get up to leave. I look at the doctor head-on for the first time, at his broad face, at the whole of him. Where do I know him from?

"And now you're going to tell me I can't come here again?"

He thrusts his hands deep into the pockets of his white coat. I envy him. I wish I were back at work. I feel so small.

"No, Nancy, I am definitely not going to do that. You care about your patient. That's why you're here, right? Well, good for you. You come and hang out as much as you like."

He doesn't get up and walk away as he should, so I have to. I stand up and head down the hospital corridor. It's a long walk before there is a corner which I can turn, to get my privacy back. The whole way down the corridor, I wonder if he is still looking at me. And even then, I don't go back to thinking about my patient. I wonder how the doctor knew my name.

* * *

"Nancy, it's not necessary to be such a complete freak, you know. I'm asking you to do the cress, not put your name down for an allotment."

My nephew's face is solemn. He puts his hand on my arm to compensate for his mother's harshness, and says, "It's not hard to do. D'you want me to show you?"

"I want to! I want to!" My niece joins in, jumping up and down, maddened by her brother who, having discovered the sudden preciousness of the seeds, is waving them above his sister's head, just out of her three-year-old reach.

Julia just crosses her arms and looks at me. It's not rocket science, says her face. You're meant to be giving me a break. I take a child's neck in each hand, sachet now in teeth. I can't believe this is enough to make them laugh. I motion with my eyes to my sister that she should leave the room, free herself. I marvel at how noisy her life is compared to my own.

Then we have the upturned lid of an egg box. My niece has filled an old Avent baby bottle, with the top of the teat chopped off. The children tear paper towels from the roll, and fold them and lay them, ever so carefully, in the lid, then make them sodden from the bottle.

Through the kitchen hatch, I see the sitting room full of the wide silver light of winter, and feel the allure of this place which is empty of children. There is the lime-green sofa and, past that, the sea, its short waves showing their olive underbellies. The spiff of foam blown sideways off them as they break.

"Aunty Nance!" calls me back to two right hands cupped for seeds. It is for me to fill these hands, a job they don't doubt I'm up to. He must be tired of female emotion, my straight-faced nephew, what with Julia and myself in the same house all weekend; impatient with the welling of tears in a grown woman's eyes. "Do you want to try?" he says, taking the seeds from me and pouring a pile in my palm. I think of the grain holder in Virginia that we tried to climb into and how angry our parents were because you could die doing that. My niece has left some space for me in their wadding bed. I find it is not quite enough for me to scatter the sharp-smelling seeds. I press them gently where they land, into the softness there.

WEEK THREE

It doesn't take me long to remember how I know David. I am reading fairy tales to my niece. The children are being led deep into the forest by their father and wicked stepmother, but Hansel is a clever boy and drops white pebbles from his pocket, making a path along which he and his sister can wend their way home again in the moonlight. Lying there on the top bunk, I am put in mind of David's boots, the crescents of mud they shed. And suddenly I think of his feet on a different floor. He is getting up from a chair in a faraway hospital and walking with purpose into one of the side rooms.

The woman in that room was a respiratory patient and should have been in a different part of the hospital, but there was no space for her so she'd been placed on our ward. The problem was that she was often forgotten. I was an intern then, and I passed her many times a day as I went about my work. And as long mornings arrived at their destination of lunchtime, while afternoons dimmed into evening, no relatives came and often no ward rounds. She didn't forget herself, though. Whenever a shadow passed her threshold, she'd call out, "Come in, please" or say, "I'm here. In here."

The smell of her also reminded us of her presence. She left lunches uneaten because she probably had no appetite. And the stink of these lunches and her disease filled the corridor of our ward, and her disease filled her small room where the window was never open. It misted and showed strange scuffs from earlier times, when greasy backs may have leaned against it, or brushed against it as nurses or doctors gave care to someone lying in the bed.

She made me feel terrible, this woman, but what could I do? I was an intern and had my own responsibilities. But this didn't stop one of the other doctors. It didn't stand in the way of David. One day, he walked onto the ward when I was sitting at the nurses' station. He went straight for the notes trolley, pulled out that woman's file and put it on the counter. He didn't notice me sitting there. He bit his nails and flipped through the notes and he looked angry, which struck me, as it seemed very daring that an intern should think it their place to exhibit any personal feelings at all.

Then he shut the folder, put it back in the trolley and did something even more brazen. He headed directly towards her, that woman who wasn't even his charge. When he strode straight into her room she looked over from the window to his face and smiled and, for a moment, I wondered if they knew each other. She held out a hand to him and he took it immediately and stood next to her like her best boy. I moved from the nurses' station to right outside the patient's door. From my watch point, I could see how her eyelashes were separate and fanned out with glee because her eyes had a reason to be wide open for the first time in ages, because someone required her attention.

"What do you need?" he asked her.

"For someone to tell me when I am going to die." She smiled and her voice was strong. She pumped his hand as she said the strong words, encouraging him: do not lose heart, my boy.

He took her hand in both of his, as I stood outside the door, watching, listening. He spoke slowly, as if by measuring out the medicine of his words in the tiniest doses he might know exactly when to stop, at precisely which point his charge might fail in her courage. I should have remembered his gentle accent from this sentence alone. Oh so slowly the words came out, in syllables.

"Your life is coming to an end."

That was all he said. And she exhaled. The more air she let out, the more her smile re-formed. She shut her eyes to allow herself this, then opened them again. Her face was full of gladness. Her voice was steady. She thanked him. It was the fullest thank-you I have ever heard: a blessing.

Might there be a way, after all, for me to tell my own difficult truth? To say everything that has happened without sinking myself in the process? Does the whole story have to be dark, just because that's how it ends?

I take the train back to London. I look through the window for answers. I study the distinct sections of land, the way the fields darken into the distance, mark where deep green meets the vast arc of orange-and-blue sky, note the tiny pylons stretching over the hill, looped together with black threads. Then I change my view and stare down at the blurring of grass right next to me and the bending and weaving of the sidings. I feel the train rock this way and that and, for a few moments, I think I have it. The truth weaves and bends along the tracks, and the colors of this evening are the shades of my American childhood, and all may still be well, because the events of recent times are lining up for me and promising to make sense.

In a summer full of rain, I summoned the courage to apply for a job as a fellow. My peers laughed at me and told me I was jumping the gun, I didn't have anything like enough experience, but they were wrong because one day I got the response I'd been dreaming of. I was called to compete for one of the two available training positions in my region. Standing by the window in my flat, I gripped the letter of invitation until my fingers made dents in it, and looked out at the courtyard where the wet weather had brought out the brightness in everything so that the paving stones shone like gunmetal and the bench stood conker-bright and the plants appeared as shiny as new limes.

What a grand new start. I would leave behind the rest of my underling class, the phalanx of unnoticed interns and junior residents, the scut-workers. I imagined myself, briefcase in hand, smartly dressed, greeting senior colleagues on the ward round. I envisaged how it would be to take my call from home, pager on my bedside table, taking messages over the phone and electing, on occasion, to drive through the brilliant empty night to my hospital where I would sweep sick patients for surgery, ease tricky babies out of their mothers, rescue women from ectopic pregnancies. I thought of the operating theater, that green heaven in which I would clear and console and sort. Where I would no longer be a bystander, but a person worthy enough to be trained to the point of absolute surgical freedom.

Determined to land that job, I did everything in my power to prepare. I cocooned myself from the sniping of my colleagues by working even harder than usual. During jobs on the wards, from under the canopy of patients' legs, I studied the way the fellows behaved as a zoologist might a new species. I took note of the things they checked each time they visited a patient, the charts and drains and wounds. I studied their manners too, their gentle authority with the nurses, their new familiarity with fellows from other specialties, their ever so slightly attenuated deference to the specialists. I looked at what they wore.

When others went to the canteen for lunch, I headed for the library and surreptitiously ate my sandwiches while reading a big book with a jazzy font called *Gems of Clinical Governance* from cover to cover. When I needed the loo, I took an extra minute there to study one of the index cards I carried in my pocket at all times, which outlined key steps for handling every emergency of my specialty. On my way home in the evening, I stopped at the municipal pool and mouthed my responses to classic interview questions, my lips billowing oddly against the chlorine, staring goggle-eyed at the steep slant of the pool's base as if I were facing my interviewers, undeterred by the plasters and occasional panty-liner I saw dotted there. On a rare weekend away from the hospital, I bought a trouser suit.

The interviews were held at a neighboring hospital, in a modern glass building with a spacious foyer, unfurnished but for one long bench. As I approached I could see a line of candidates sitting there, the girls dressed hot like secretaries, the guys as tense as traders in their suits. I even recognized one or two. But I knew that if I joined them I would lose some of my nerve so, instead of heading for the bench, I ducked around the corner of the building where I wouldn't be seen, and stood with my back to the wall to gain what shelter I could from the rain which fell relentlessly.

It was minutes before I noticed that someone else had had the same idea, before I turned at some small noise to see Jay, another doctor from my own hospital, standing a few meters away, side on to the building, one narrow leg crossed over the other. He came towards me, stepping into the rain to pass by and, momentarily, he faced me head-on. Rain fell on him and he smiled.

"You're a better doctor than all those nitwits in there," he said. "I've seen you."

And then he sauntered off. I watched him until he disappeared around the corner, poof, just like that, leaving me with a sense of buoyancy and confidence I had not felt five minutes earlier.

It's no wonder, really, that Jay opens this story, the tale of Nancy-the-Brave, as my train chunters through the dusk towards London. No surprise that this young man—a force to be reckoned with, that's what people are always saying about him—should come to mind as I gaze out at the elements of earth and sky. As my train begins to slow, and other passengers start to gather their coats and close their books and shift themselves, ready to alight, I stay quite still because I don't want to disrupt memory and what it seems to promise. I want it to unravel itself, optimistically, all the way to its natural end. When we finally come to a halt, I don't immediately get off the train, but think instead of coming out of that glass building, into whose interview room I had been called back and offered a fellow post. Stepping out into the evening which I had already marked as the first evening of the rest of my life, I saw an elegant man standing there, waiting patiently for me, as if the two jobs had been ours all along.

Those first few months were as exciting as they were scary. My time was split more or less evenly between the two subspecialties, gynecology and obstetrics, with on-call nights bridging the two. On an average day, I would turn up extra early to do a quick check of the really sick patients before my interns arrived for the ward round. After ensuring they each had a list of things that needed to be done before the end of play, I would head off to clinic or theater.

Before my promotion, I had always scorned obstetrics as the lesser of the two disciplines. "Babies can get born by themselves," I would say. Or I would blithely join in with the institutional mockery of the "madwives," that population of nurses we accused of taking pleasure in providing any obstruction they could to a woman getting proper pain relief in labor, who certainly had nothing to teach us. How I regretted my ignorance now. I soon saw that pregnancies could become disastrous at absolutely any stage. There were eclampsia and gestational diabetes and sickle-cell disease to look out for. Women contracted catastrophic infections and single-organ malfunctions and there was an entire compendium of complications associated with carrying twins. Then there were the really scary problems, placenta previa, placental abruption, uterine rupture—bloody events that could result in the death of mother as well as child. And all this before a woman even went into labor.

Realizing how much I had to learn, I abandoned pride. I didn't think twice about phoning the attending physician in the middle of the night if I was unsure what to do when I was on call, often summoning them to the hospital when distant advice didn't seem enough and disregarding their impatient looks as they arrived in theater dressed incongruously in civvies.

I also started to make good the cavernous gaps in my knowledge. In the evenings, I read about every obstetric problem known to man, starting with the most worrying and working my way down the list. On days off, I went to the antenatal clinic and cast myself on the mercy of the midwives there who, over a period of months, supervised me while I honed skills I ought already to have been slick at. How to use a Pinard stethoscope, the best way to measure symphyseal-fundal height, assessing fetal lie. In short, what a normal pregnancy looked like and how to monitor its development.

Gynecology came more easily to me and I was as happy sitting in clinic, taking histories from the women there, as I had been anywhere in my life. It reminded me of when, as a child, I had been taught in music lessons how to separate strands of sound one from another, how to listen to a piece of piano-playing and be able to sing back to the teacher either line from the combined score, the treble or bass. In this altogether different setting I began to see that the words a patient uttered were not always what counted most; that there might be a more important meaning beyond what was being said, a contrary melody, if only I could train my ear to hear it.

As for my surgical training, I was assigned for my first six months to a general gynecologist called Dr. Kapoor. We spent two days a week in the OR, and he started to teach me the bread-and-butter techniques of my field. I was grateful to have been placed with this specialist. He was a quiet, unassuming figure, the least macho man I'd ever met in a pair of scrubs. And, best of all, he was happy for me to get involved, evacuating vulval hematomas, cauterizing cervical erosion, examining uteruses under anesthetic, and plenty more besides. Cack-handed though I was at the outset, I sensed my boss was happy with me. I was punctual, hardworking and didn't have a squeamish bone in my body.

Jay, on the other hand, was already making a name for himself. All over the hospital, people were talking. The best pair of hands in a generation. A surgical prodigy. He had been seconded to a job where his time was split between the guy who did most of the department's cancer work and the Assisted Conception Unit, an elegant glass building financed by donations from a millionaire and renowned for keeping the rest of the hospital financially afloat. On a ward round one morning, I overheard an intern saying Jay had been allowed to choose embryos for transfer the previous day, a task usually performed only by the specialist. I was eager to ask him all about it myself, though the truth was that we were both so busy now we didn't see so much of each other.

As it happened, I did bump into Jay that week. Early for the OR one morning, I stopped by the surgical coffee room for a drink and found him sitting there. The only other person in the room was one of the orthopedic surgeons, reading a magazine: legs splayed, dark scrubs tucked into white, calf-high boots adorned with the intricate tracery of bloodwork.

I took a cup from the cupboard and raised it to Jay in an offer of tea, which he declined. He put the journal he had been reading into his briefcase as I sat down opposite him.

"So, what's on?" I asked.

"Ovarian tumor. Big one," he said. "Hoping to get my hands dirty."

"Great." I picked up my mug of tea, which was still too hot even to sip. Steam collected in the hairs of my upper lip as I held it to my mouth. I waited for Jay to ask what my morning had in store. Across the room, the orthopod shook the magazine he was holding in one hand to make its pages stand to attention. I blew an eddy of steam across my cup. Eventually, I spoke again.

"And the ACU. How's that going? Are you magicking babies from thin air yet?"

Jay frowned. But then he sat forward, and rested his forearms on his knees, his face keen again and as open as a little boy's. His eyes shone, dark all over and glossy like nuts.

"It's incredible, Nancy. Really. You wouldn't believe

the things we're doing up there. Truly groundbreaking things. It's not just helping women with their fertility, you know. It's like we're giving them their freedom!"

Of course I had learned something of this too, from my own side of the fence, this business of granting women control over their own bodies. But, after waiting a few moments, I realized Jay wasn't going to ask me about my work. So I said, "I'd better get going," rose and emptied my tea in the sink, untouched. As the door that I had pulled open began to swing back I thought suddenly that I had been harsh on my friend and turned round to say goodbye. But what I saw through the narrowing space left by the closing door made me change my mind. Jay's back was to me now and the orthopod wasn't reading his magazine. He had looked up and was facing Jay. And I could see clearly that a joke was already breaking between them.

But this was an isolated incident. Mainly, we carried on as before, often sharing the on-call pager, not because we couldn't handle a whole night of work ourselves but because neither of us wanted to miss out on any of the action. They were happy days, whichever way I chose to cut it. After those call nights, we'd gather in the doctors' mess, fellows from every hospital specialty. Sitting on the sofas with tea and toast, Jay still somehow managing to look as fresh as a daisy, everyone would tell stories about what they'd seen and done during the course of the night. As my companions talked, I would look out of the window beyond their heads and study the colors of dawn forming in the sky and the crenellation of buildings below, in the darkness. And I would feel complete, my appetite for conversation already sated by the events of the night. I concluded that if my life didn't change one iota, it would be a happy one.

At times, I can't help thinking about how things would have panned out if Jay and I had started off in each other's jobs. Whether our respective fates, my failure and his success, were sealed by a simple roll of the secretarial dice. But mostly I just wonder where he is now, my stellar friend. How much progress he has made in these past few weeks, while I have stood stock-still.

Julia's fond of saying I did my first abortion with my eyes half shut. That I never signed up for the events that dominate my life now. It makes her angry that no one ever sat me down and asked explicitly whether I wanted to learn how to perform a termination. And of course, I see her point. It is surprising, with all the namby-pamby talk in the medical world these days, the communication skills this, and cultural diversity that, that no such discussion ever took place.

But, in another sense, it all seems pretty academic. Because I know one thing for sure. If I ever had been asked, if some kind of open forum had existed at which fellows had been invited to take a line on the subject, I could only ever have gone one way. Not only because, like every other civilized person I knew, I agreed with abortion on principle. But because, once upon a time, I had needed one myself.

I knew what color the paint was inside the Marie Stopes clinic near Victoria Station. I knew what it was like to walk in there and be stared at by everyone in the reception room. I knew how it was to feel like a fool and a fraud for not having better reasons for making my solemn request. It was in that place, not my own hospital department, that I had seen my first HSA1, the single-sided blue form on which each woman's reasons for wanting to terminate her pregnancy are inscribed. There that I had given my blood and lain down for a scan. There that I had bartered for the abortion of my own fetus, not hesitating for a heartbeat to agree, when asked, that I believed my mental health would deteriorate significantly if I continued with my pregnancy. And, you know, a person can't have a thing like that in their life, and just edit it out.

For the first few months, I only did the occasional abortion, just as they happened to crop up on Dr. Kapoor's general cases, among all the other gynecological procedures I was becoming a dab hand at. But the day came when my boss asked me if I'd be interested in doing more. Maybe he told me that the department was snowed under with work. Or perhaps it was that an opportunity had arisen for a keen young fellow wanting to make their mark. I don't remember the introduction. But I do remember the deal. For one day per fortnight I would get my own termination clinic in the morning, followed by the OR in the afternoon. Real independence with the safety net of a specialist working nearby at all times. All I needed to do to sign up was go and see Frederick.

And that was how I found myself in his office for the first time. High up on the fourth floor one sunny afternoon, with the windows open and the sun shining in and the radio on. Being served tea by the most unlikely specialist I had ever met, a man with a ponytail and multicolored trousers. Sitting on his sofa beneath a wall full of baby pictures and thank-you cards from all the couples he had seen in the Assisted Conception Unit and hearing some of their stories. Eating biscuits and watching Frederick pace about his office, oblivious to the papers fluttering across his desk by the wide-open window as he expounded on his equal commitment to providing abortion and fertility services. Two sides of the same coin, was how he saw it.

I still like the way Frederick didn't separate abortion out from everything else. Because, in some ways, it is no different to any other kind of surgery. Not easier or harder, not more gory or more disgusting. Every surgeon picks the organ they will spend the whole of their career protecting. The neurosurgeon gets the brain, the colorectal surgeon the bowel. And we gynecologists have the womb to look after. A piece of tissue as small as a fist but with the capacity to expand and fill the whole abdomen. An organ with great tensile strength but delicate as paper and as easy to perforate. And whichever specialty we choose, each of us has to do something ruthless to keep our patients safe. We have to forget about the human significance of the organ we are operating on. So this is what I do. Before each abortion, I tell myself that the precise contents of my patient's womb cannot be my concern. The fetus is merely the potentially treacherous surgical field in which I am working, while my patient, the person whom I have made myself absolute protector of, sleeps her sleep.

And there's something else I want my judges to know. I have derived great satisfaction from becoming expert in this procedure. From knowing exactly which dilator to choose for which cervix. From the sixth sense I have developed about the angle of each uterus. From my growing confidence in knowing how far to go to empty the womb safely but without damaging it, so that it might serve its owner well in other, happier circumstances. I am proud of the work I have done.

But the story doesn't stick. All night long, the wind bellows down the empty communal corridors of my home and, in the morning, I wake from a dream in which I am sitting in theater, face blank as a canvas, blood dripping from my hands. Except it isn't a dream. It's the real, final act in my short adventure as a doctor. And, as such, any version of events I concoct has to lead directly up to it. I stare out of the window, down to the courtyard which is strewn with branches and green leaves, and I wonder suddenly whether it was all bound to happen. Wasn't I always a passive little wretch? Even as a child, I never could say no. Maybe that bloody surgical scene was the last of a long string of mistakes. Perhaps each moment of disastrous inaction could have been detected in the one before it. Silence giving birth to silence, one missed opportunity to save myself after another.

It's not as if that last day came out of the blue. I went to see Frederick weeks before the end. I didn't mull over exactly what I'd say when I got there, I just woke up after yet another of those dream-filled nights and knew I couldn't go on as I was. I remember how out of breath I was as I climbed the stairs to his office. Tired. Nervous about how I would articulate what I hardly understood myself. None of the other fellows talk to me anymore. I believe but I don't believe. I want to carry on, because this is the most important thing

I've ever done in my life—but I think I'll have to quit because it's making me ill.

When I reached Frederick's office, I found the door open but no one there. I stood on the threshold. Papers fluttered across the desk, spilling onto the floor as the wind blew through the open window. Two teacups sat on the table by the sofa, small brown puddles in their bases. A hundred pairs of babies' eyes stared at me from the photo display on the wall. I crossed the room and lowered the sash. I stood for a moment or two, not knowing what to do next and looked out at the Day Surgery Unit, three stories below.

A few minutes later, I was standing beneath its great porch. I passed through the waiting room and up the stairs to change into scrubs. I headed for theater. I didn't go through the normal door, though, the one that would bring me right to him. I entered through the anesthetic room, so that I would come in near the patient's head. I wanted to look at her face. I hoped it would give me courage.

What a cool blue room. What a background for such redness. The radio blared unhelpful songs. "When I Kissed the Teacher." "Rude Boy." The anesthetic assistant stood in his usual position to one side, ultrasound probe resting on the patient's distended belly. Beyond her outstretched legs, I saw Frederick, hair pulled back under his surgical cap, neck and arm sinews stretched with effort beyond the green drape. The bowl not visible, the ultrasound not visible, the work not visible.

It wouldn't have taken much. It would have been enough to have said just a few words. Hello, colleague. What a fine day it is outside. But not in here. I simply cannot bear to stand alongside you and watch what you are doing. Perhaps he saw it in my face. I didn't need to speak: Frederick filled the silence instead. If only our doubters would bother to find out about these women's stories, Nancy. I think we'd change their minds, don't you? Take this lady. Twenty-two weeks' gestation. Recent diagnosis of breast cancer, aggressive type. If she keeps the baby, she dies. And, even after this, she'll need the whole deal. Surgery, radio, chemo.

I inched closer to him. He talked me into his orbit. But it isn't just the women with cancer, is it, Nancy? Not just those whose babies are growing without kidneys or brains. It isn't just the rape victims or the abused ones. They're not the only cases with merit. They're just the ones whose sad stories are the easiest to fathom.

By now, I was standing next to him, at the heart of his justification. This is what our arms worked so strenuously for. To help others whom no one else would give relief. For the good. And soon, I found it wasn't too awful after all to stand next to my boss. To look into the bowl in front of me and confront the sight of absolute brokenness there.

I've asked myself the question a hundred times. Why didn't I speak up that day? Why didn't I try harder to make myself understood? I could have saved a woman's life if I had stepped out of the ring in time. I could have saved myself. But I think I understand now what I felt that afternoon. The bald fact of it. Which is that some acts can never be undone. It's not possible to un-become a killer. Once you have ended a life, you cannot walk back over that line, however blindly you may have crossed it.

There was nothing unusual about the way that first day began. Nothing odd in the weather, nothing strange or silent when I stepped out of my flat that morning to go work in the OR with Dr. Kapoor. No single magpies, or broken mirrors or swirls of smoke. The bus came on time and I don't remember a single soul on it. I didn't commit to memory the faces of the people who saw me just before I made the biggest moral leap of my life.

I don't remember anything particular about my passage through the hospital either, though I must have taken those last innocent steps past the cashpoint machine, up to the first floor and towards the theater suite. There would have been a receptionist sitting there, even at such an early hour, and perhaps she wished me a cheerful good morning, the last warm, pure, unsuspicious greeting I would ever have from someone sitting at that desk.

In my mind's eye, my footsteps etch a red track. I see myself walking towards my fate. I stop at the scrubs shelves and select my surgical attire. I take top and bottoms into the women's changing room and, a few minutes later, I am out again. Transformed for my work. Keen and ready to go although there is nothing indecent about this hunger. It is just another day at the hospital.

I meet my boss at the noticeboard. Good morning, Dr. Kapoor. It must still be the first few weeks of my apprenticeship for me to address him this formally. We look together at what the day has in store. The OR case list does not say Hazard. It does not say Go Home, Young Surgeon, or Beware. There is just a column of short procedures: ERPC, D & C, ToP, EUA, insertion of IUD. Dr.

Kapoor decodes them for me. He tells me there will be plenty for me to do. He extends his hand out to the side, a chivalrous gesture, and points me in the right direction. Look at me now, the jejune trainee, all puffed up with pride, leading the way. A pool of blood already collecting around my feet, if only I could see it.

In theater, I wait on a stool. Dr. Kapoor opens his briefcase on his lap and attends to some papers. I hear the anesthesiologist, in the room next door, greeting our first patient. I take out my surgical logbook and open it. Its leaves are blank and white. A *tabula rasa*. I look at the page in front of me. *Core Module 15: Sexual and Reproductive Health.* There is a list of procedures beneath the heading, skills I need to master. And there is something else: a footnote in tiny font which says "Please mark conscientious objection (CO) alongside skills not acquired." What can this mean? I scan the list again to see what act a person might possibly want to abstain from. I see Termination of Pregnancy.

This is the warning. This is the signal. Here is the moment of great commotion. There is blood pouring down the walls. The room is a river of blood. The walls shake and trumpets blast and drums roll. I must be deaf and blind to hear and see nothing of this. I ignore the sign, although it is so very clear.

I look back at the footnote and at the serious words there. Conscientious objection. It seems a fat phrase. I sit there quietly on my stool and I think of the pacifist, arguing against his own conscription. The very thought feels anachronistic. A question forms in my mind: Is there a difference between conscientiously objecting to doing something and conscientiously objecting to something being done? But I don't get the chance to think about it.

Suddenly, the room is all action. The double doors bang open. The patient is wheeled into the center of the room. People cluster round to move her onto the table. One, two, three, over. This is what a person becomes a doctor for. Nurses unfurl drapes. The bottom section of the bed is cracked loose from its hinges. The monitor blinks and the patient's legs are up in stirrups. A pack of instruments clatters on to a trolley. I approach the bed in my gown and mask and all the loud and moving things become still around me. My boss watches as I lower my weight onto the stool the nurse pushes forward. I am pinpoint-focused.

ERPC. Evacuation of the retained products of conception. I clean my patient's pudendum. Miscarriage at thirteen weeks. Some retained products on ultrasound. My hand hovers over the instruments. I select a cannula to suit the size of my patient's cervix. The nurse turns on the suction and I introduce my instrument, using it to gently sweep the uterus, to empty it of its contents and stop it bleeding. Good job, says Dr. Kapoor when I am finished. Do the next one too.

D & C. Dilatation and curettage. Exactly the same as before, just differently named because of its different indication. Last time, a miscarriage. This time, heavy periods. I finish the second case. Well done, but make sure you're thorough, says my boss. He nods for me to scrub again as he talks. What you see on the ultrasound screen is no substitute for what you have to learn to sense with your hands. A scratchy feeling against the curette tip that tells you if the uterus is empty. Here, show me. He nods to the operating table, where our third patient is already waiting.

ToP. Termination of pregnancy. I know which patient this is. I know what she is having done. I look at Dr. Kapoor, to gauge the loaded expectation in his face but find his expression blank. Everything else is just the same as before. The anesthesiologist reads his paper. The scrub nurse stands by the trolley. The radio plays quiet classics. I breathe in and I breathe out. Just for a second, I pause. Something in me stretches and arcs. And then, the moment is gone. My assistant squirts jelly on the woman's abdomen and applies the probe there. I soak a swab-on-a-stick with chlorhexidine. All the moments run together quite smoothly again. I have placed the Sims speculum in the introitus and opened the vagina. I am visualizing the cervix. I attach vulsellum forceps to the cervical lip and select a Hegar dilator. I am putting in the suction curette.

There is nothing in the mechanics of what I do to distinguish this procedure from the two I have done before it. Not the size of the cannula. Nor the time it takes to complete the job. Not the small amount of blood which empties discreetly along the tubing into a closed drain by my feet. Not the sanitary towel I press against my patient when I am finished. Not the sparse conversation I have with my boss. Nothing whatsoever that might indicate to a young woman that she has just made the biggest mistake of her life.

I am walking out of my flat to get the bus, when I suddenly change my mind. I go back indoors and struggle out of my suit. Leaving it lying on the floor, I quickly re-dress in trousers and a jumper. I take the lift to the basement and, after rummaging around for ten minutes, haul out the bicycle I inherited from my mum. Mint green, straight handles, light frame. Is superstition all I have left? Some flimsy notion that, by sitting in my mother's saddle, I'll intuit what she might have advised me. How to approach my last panel, in what manner to put things to my judges, which of the many explanations I have come up with is the most authentic.

The sky is fresh and blue up above my block of flats, but the street is still cast in shadow, a deep cold gray. I pull the collar of my jumper up around my neck, and the sleeves down over my hands. I push off the curb and change into third gear straightaway, eager to feel my body do something that feels like work.

Soon, I am speeding along the Embankment, looking for clues. I turn alternative stories over in my mind, trying each one against the world around me. Beech trees line the pavement in front of the smartest of houses. It is hard not to believe that everything will be all right, looking at all this bright stucco, the window boxes full of blinding red and blue. A whole row of houseboats passes me on my right. For a second, a man is spraying his deck with a hose, then my face is full of lime-bright leaves and I am cycling through the embrace of trees.

I reach the bridge. Up its slope I pedal, to its gentle summit, and look down onto the muddy, dimpled banks of the Thames, chocolate-brown in the glare. I see a couple beneath me in waders, mud larks, foraging in the grime. I freewheel down the bridge into the sun's full rays, which pick out the dirt in the air and cracked paint on buildings, and the fumes from cars and the glint of litter. I alternate tales again to see which one fits best here, and it is not the same as before.

Finally, I arrive at the hospital. The huge building rears up, center stage. For the monumental task ahead I must pull myself back into the concrete world from the blankness of pedaling and the empty wind of my journey. From the details all around me, which might so easily sabotage reason. The low hum of the automatic door opening and shutting to let people in and out. A mother shouting in the car park to her child. A family gathered tightly round a man in a wheelchair telling jokes. The alarm on a supplies lorry—out of the way, blind people!—reversing into its allocated slot.

I find a place to lock my bike. I fix the front wheel to a black cycle-stand, and when I stand up, someone is right next to me. David.

"I wanted to wish you luck." He wears a new white coat over his clothes. I can see the creases in it from when it was square in its plastic pack. "Actually that's not quite true." He pushes his hands deep into his pockets. "What I really wanted was to ask you out for a drink."

I look down. After a while I say, "Your boots. They drop mud."

A couple walk past me. First floor, the man explains to his companion. Turn right, second on the right. I envisage the orthopedic ward. When I look up at David, he seems amused. "Why do Santa's little helpers wear seat belts?" he says. And then, apologetically, "Elfin safety."

I smile, and this is all he needs. He throws his head back and laughs, so loudly that all the people outside the hospital turn and look at him. He is still laughing as I turn away and walk towards the tall doors of the hospital's main entrance, and on to where my judges await me.

Everything is going smoothly.

"One day you were operating safely," says Dr. Mansfield. "Then you weren't. What happened that day? Can we satisfy ourselves it was an aberration? Or is the problem more serious? Can we fix it and, if so, how? This is what we have to cover in the next hour."

I look from one to the other. Dr. Garber has opened the folder in front of him and has already started to read from my CV. "Graduated with honors in surgery as well as obstetrics and gynecology. Tons of publications. Recent presentation at a national meeting. Strongest candidate at interview."

"Ah yes, the interview." This upbeat, merry voice is my own. "The things I was asked. One manager wanted me to list the seven pillars of Clinical Governance. Like it's some kind of monument! Well, fortunately for me, I had a mnemonic. PIRATES. Patient and public involvement. Information and IT. Risk management. Audit. Training. Effectiveness and Staff management." I count them off on confident fingers. "I mean, can you imagine what the general public, what *patients* would think if they knew this is the kind of stuff doctors are being tested on, to see if they're good enough to become hospital specialists!"

We all laugh. The four of us are smiling together.

"Shall I tell you about my first abortion?"

"No!" says Dr. Garber. He stands up from his chair,

hand raised. He looks like someone trying to stop a high-speed train.

It's the GP's turn again.

"How did you feel immediately after doing that first abortion?"

"Fine."

"Fine?"

"Yes."

"Not shaky? Or upset?"

"No."

"Well, I suppose that makes sense. I mean, you must have had strong personal reasons for signing up to do terminations in the first place."

"I didn't sign up."

"But I'm right in saying you didn't exactly opt out either? You didn't conscientiously object?"

"No."

"So, you must have felt pretty strongly? Not to conscientiously object?"

"Must I?"

"Didn't you?"

"Yes."

"You did? Or you didn't?"

"I did. I do. I believe in abortion. I absolutely do."

I can hear a tapping sound.

Perhaps the lullaby effect of a story will stop them interrupting me.

"It was in the very early days of my ob-gyn training, and my sister had invited me to stay. Only, when I got there, I saw there were others too. An unfamiliar car parked outside, a couple I'd never met before, just sitting down at the kitchen table as I came in with my bags. And a baby, in one of those wheelie things, pushing itself around the floor. My sister made everything right, though. She sat us all down, my brother-in-law brought out the tea, and soon the husband-guest, a man called Simon, was asking me about my journey.

"Then Julia went to the kitchen and got one of her fantastic cakes. A lovely Victoria sponge, which was super-high, not miserable and flat the way mine always turn out. And we all stopped talking to admire the cake and Julia cut everyone a piece. Soon we were all sitting round with these slabs of cake in front of us and it was then that the wife said, 'Your sister was telling us you're training to be an obstetrician and gynecologist. What a fascinating job. It must be so rewarding being present at all those births.'

"And I agreed, but I felt cross too. Because it always annoys me when people think that childbirth is the most interesting part of the job we do. So I replied that I had always preferred the other side of the specialty, gynecology.

"My sister went to fetch more water for the tea and Simon inquired which area of gynecology that was, the bit I was doing at that particular time. I said I was in the middle of a module on Contraception and Sexually Transmitted Diseases and I only had to start mentioning these phrases for the wife to start eating her cake in quite a specific, careful way. And then, looking at her husband, but asking me the question, she said, 'Does that mean you sometimes refer women for abortions?'

"This made me a bit wild. So I let her have it. I said,

'It doesn't work that way, you know. There isn't just some person out there, separate from the rest of the world, to whom we can refer women with difficult problems. That's not really what being a doctor is all about. That person is an obstetrician-gynecologist. And helping women with unwanted pregnancies is part of our job, our duty. Not just those who have everything under control, but also the ones who are in a mess. Helping them end their pregnancies, if that's what they need to do.'

"And then, just as Julia came back into the room with the kettle, the woman turned her full face on me and said, 'What? Do you mean to say you actually *do* abortions?' And I said, 'Yes.' "

I look at my judges for any small sign of support. Dr. Mansfield rests the ball of her pen on her page. Dr. Garber clears his throat.

"Then my sister sat down next to me, and put her arm around me. And she was so understanding, you know," I say, looking directly at the three judges. "She told me how brave she thought I was, right in front of her guests," I tell my judges, not taking my eyes off them. "And do you know what I thought?" I look at each doctor in front of me in turn. "I thought that there was no way I'd be able to explain to these people, who had probably already made their minds up, how I had come to do my first termination. That no one had ever given me the luxurious scope for outrage that I was expected to grant others. That the experience of being in an operating theater doing these procedures was quite different to that of hearing oneself talk about it while eating Victoria sponge. That I would never be able to explain to them how complicated it is to be a doctor."

I realize where the sound is coming from. It's the young woman Vivien's foot. She is tapping it against her chair.

There is the tiny beep of a digital alarm. Dr. Mansfield reaches forward to where her watch sits on the desk in front of her and presses a gold button on its side. She has her own set of questions. None of them stick in my mind. All her inquiries seem to be directed at trying to get me to say that I have not had enough support from my seniors. That I was thrown in at the deep end too early. That Frederick and Dr. Kapoor are to blame for what has happened.

Anger fills the room. The sound of it dances around me. The Occupational Health lady looks straight ahead. Her cheeks are aflame. I can hear her foot, still knocking against the leg of her chair, but much more loudly now. Her eyes are the prettiest violet. Garber and Mansfield face each other closely. Their words are like one sentence.

"Just admit it, Miriam?" He pokes his finger at her. "She lost faith!"

"That's ridiculous, Tim! You're putting words in her mouth. It's totally out of order!"

The hour passes in the blink of an eye. I leave the seminar room and go down the stairs, cross over the main corridor and continue. As I walk, I look up at the huge photos on the wall depicting important members of the hospital staff. The beaming pediatric specialist who never smiles in real life. The good-looking radiologist who taught us how to read chest X-rays at medical school. One of the newfangled nurse-practitioners, standing proudly next to her medical colleagues. The head chef of the hospital canteen, because we are all the same in this establishment, Joe Public, don't you worry. We all stand shoulder to shoulder.

It is only when I reach the foyer outside the ICU and the Step-Down Unit that I remember what I have been told. My patient is finally getting better. This is why I have come here. So that I can be close to her. I want to be near where nurses are taking tubes out of her arms and mouth. I want to imagine the incremental improvements in her physiology, the tiny clinical freedoms, the gradual healing, the body's forgiveness. I look around for somewhere to sit, but all the chairs are taken, and the thoroughfare is as busy as a supermarket. The only other place is the Relatives' Room, a place where families usually congregate for bad news. Finding it empty, I let myself in.

More care is taken in this room than in most of the hospital waiting areas. There are upright chairs and low-slung chairs to suit all sorts: those who would rather brace against disaster and those who would collapse into it. Some of the plants are real and properly tended to, and the magazines are tidy. There is even a water machine. I help myself to a drink and cross to the far side of the room.

Outside, the sky lies low over the hospital. It is as light as it's going to get and still raining hard. Down at pavement level, people cluster under trees and cigarette shelters, peering up hopefully at the sky. I see garish colors in the misty wet and imagine the swishing of mackintosh sleeves as I watch the tops of umbrellas moving in the rain, obscuring the people holding them. I see faces in hoods, rain rictuses showing what they might look like in moments of extremity.

My thoughts turn to my patient. I try to recall something exact about her. I cast my mind back to the names on the board that fateful morning, but nothing comes to me. I remember sitting on the stool in the operating theater, patients being wheeled in, one after another, pale legs raised. This pudendum shaved, that one not. I envisage the different feet. Dirty toes with fluff-packed nails. Foolish girls' feet with nails in scarlet and coral. Mothers' heels all hardened and flat.

I consider all the girls who have come to see me over the months in clinic. Their polite postures and tight little scripts. Each one with her own scant argument, just enough to earn a mark on the blue page, and no more. My pad of HSA1s, thick as a slab. I search for something more specific and the feeling of searching is not new to me. Girls swarm around my mind. Fragments of stories jostle for primacy, but they are mainly Frederick's, always the most dramatic ones, those he told me from his time in Africa. The corpses he bagged up, babies halfway out. The girl brought in by her dad, her whole bowel in a plastic bag, cut out accidentally with a pair of scissors. I try intently to access something from my own clinical experience. Surely I can remember one woman or girl? There must be someone whose details stand out, someone whose circumstances I can individuate? But all that comes to me is a memory of myself.

I am in my flat and I am bleeding. The light is strange outside. It is midmorning, but darkish, with fog all around and the empty shade of winter. I go to the loo to check on what is happening and a great brightness there alarms the dim day. I wonder if I should shout or call an ambulance.

I take the bus to the hospital. In the emergency department I am put in a cubicle and wait a long time. A nurse asks who I would like her to call, but there isn't anyone. Finally a doctor comes and instructs me to let my legs fall apart, as if this is what women's legs would naturally do if only we would let them; at least women like me, at least legs like these. Our dialogue shrinks further so that his remark is soon just the spinning of a speculum's screw, my response the creaking of my underwired bra as I lie back to accommodate him. The doctor tells me I am having a miscarriage. He doesn't bother to say sorry. He can see what a mess I am.

Suddenly the door to the Relatives' Room opens and a woman strides in, talking loudly on a mobile phone. I move away from the window and pick up a magazine. I find a seat in the corner.

"The operation? Four weeks ago today. Exactly."

I look up. The woman has crossed to where I was standing before and is looking out of the window. She's slim. She is wearing a dark-pink puffer vest with a gray jumper underneath.

"No, Jennifer. That's the thing I just don't get. Not a soul. Well, of course, someone must have. That's right. But not me, nor her father, obviously. She didn't even tell John."

I study her intently now, this tall graceful lady. Is it possible that this is my patient's mother? I pick out the

North Face logo on her anorak. I try to establish what her daughter might look like. The woman takes her free hand from her pocket and rests it on the dirty windowsill. There are lines on the back of it and I notice she is shaking.

"Yes, well, Anthony has done that already. It was pretty much the first thing he did do, actually. Although I'm not sure it's right. Yes, well, that's how he does feel. It's typical of him. But I don't know, really. I suppose all I want to do is put all my energy into helping Emily."

No wonder I have fallen apart. No wonder I have ended up poleaxed by the thought of the other living thing in my operating theater, its image being drawn into focus on the ultrasound screen, its trivial stature less noticeable than the daintiness of its distinguishable human form, its posture so touching, its heart lighting up among all the grainy black and gray.

When I look up, the woman is gone. And in the silence she leaves behind, I understand something quite clearly. I have done much worse than not articulating the particularities of my own experience. I have been deaf to those of my patients.

WEEK FOUR

It isn't steady hands that qualify the brilliant surgeon. A compassionate heart doesn't distinguish the excellent GP from his ponderous colleague. Able psychiatrists aren't mind readers any more than talented dermatologists are born to read diseases from the maps of our skin. What a doctor needs, to be good in any specialty, is a quiet appetite for the truth. The physician's gift is to sort sense from the patient's crowded somatic experience; the surgeon's challenge to detect the melody of disease in the body's cacophonous score. And, after this, a doctor has to be able to articulate what they have discovered, persuade their team of the accuracy of the diagnosis, in order that a plan for treatment and cure can be arrived at.

As I travel on the train to my sister's, for the last time before I receive the verdict of my Fitness-to-Practice Trial, all I can think of is my own failure, my inability to perform these most rudimentary therapeutic functions. I have not even started to understand my patients' truths, and I have not been able to tell my own. As I hurtle towards the conclusion of my story, I wonder what kind of doctor I am, after all, and how I deserve to be judged.

There is no one in my carriage to distract me. It is the middle of the day. Normal people are at work. The fields and towns I pass are too familiar to breed new meanings. Is there any defense for how little I have gleaned from my abortion patients, for how bald the clinical discourse over which I have presided has been? Is it conceivable that I am not wholly responsible, that some stories are just too hard for people to tell? Do certain facts have to struggle to find the circumstances in which they can be spoken? Are there secrets so delicate that they seek a special audience? Is it too much to hope that there has been a degree of recompense, that if my patients had no real opportunity to talk to me—recounting the mere skeletons of stories, the bare bones required for an abortion's purchase—each individual woman's secret tale might have been whispered somewhere else, at length, endlessly and without shame, into an understanding ear, in the generous company of a mother or friend, a lover or husband, or even hand-on-stomach to that small life she knew she could not manage to support?

And if each difficult story is just searching for the right occasion to be uttered, might this explain why, as I travel towards my sister, I feel gathering within me for the very first time the events of my own huge mistake, arranging themselves and becoming organized, gaining momentum and sense, as if all my attempts to explain myself have been no more than a rehearsal, all the comments I have made before my judges nothing more than a warming up for this purposeful burgeoning? Is that why I feel a great desire to shape the facts into something that might seem like a kind of harmony, at least when prepared for a dear sister's ear? What then will I say to Julia? How do I truly remember that most terrible day, where all this started, which was dreadful from its very dawning?

The night before my ruin, I slept badly. Just before my alarm went off, I dreamed that it was already morning, and that I awoke in my bedroom and looked out of the window to find the courtyard and gardens jet black. There were black wolves pacing around, as if the stones themselves were coming alive. Some slipped into the building, and I could hear their nails clicking as they ascended the stairs and came into the corridor outside my flat, where several were already sniffing next to my door. I woke up shaken and threw open the window and made tea and sat in bed with it. It was restless weather. The air was gusty and damp, and the eaves of the building moaned. I felt afraid, all by myself in my room, and impatient to be on my way, to get into the clean, silent space of my operating theater, where I was better accustomed to keeping my feelings at bay.

I caught the bus in the lonely morning and no one got on or off, and the monstrous vehicle rolled and swayed over the bridge, faster than a bus should. Soon, I was stepping into the other world, out into the reek of fast food from the high street. People were everywhere, despite the early hour, crowding around the main entrance of the hospital. And that morning, I was aware that the accents around me were not those of my family and friends; when I did meet someone's eye, I wanted to turn from them because they looked mad, or had an angry dog. The paving I turned my eyes down to was stained with all sorts of filth, with butts and gum and foul sputum. The only beauty was in the faraway sky which felt more distant there than it had at home. My heart felt sick at what my hands were about to do.

Inside the Day Surgery Unit, things were as usual. On one side of the high wooden reception counter were the baleful general public, waiting to check in. Pristine, entitled staff sat on the other. I noticed again the private apartheid I had been aware of for months now between me and all the other doctors. The frosty nod I got from the receptionist compared to the warm smile she gave the orthopedic fellow coming through the door just after me, the assistance the nurses conspicuously withheld from me as I shuffled through the trolley of notes to find the patients whose consents I needed for that morning's OR case list.

Arriving at the whiteboard, I saw that two of my patients had canceled so that there were only five cases for me to get through, all under ten weeks' gestation. An easy morning, I thought just before I saw May, the anesthesiologist, coming out from behind one of the curtains.

"Looks like fate's smiling on us today." She approached me, beaming at a row of nurses as she crossed the room before lowering her voice to add, "Only a few to do, and no one's fat or tricky." Then she looked at my face more closely. "Hey, you don't look too good. New man? Burning the candle at both ends?"

For a moment, I thought I might cry. I squeezed May's arm and said I'd see her in theater, before grabbing a handful of yellow forms and all the slim sets of patient notes and heading off towards the series of shut curtains behind which I knew my patients were waiting.

I consented the five of them fast. Their ages ranged from fourteen to forty. In affect, they occupied the usual ground between nervous and surly. Two had undergone terminations of pregnancy in the past, and didn't need anything explained. Another had given birth to one child by Caesarean section. The remaining ones were straight-forward. I was satisfied with my interaction with each of them, although I cannot believe now that it felt adequate to me.

Upstairs in the locker room, I changed quickly. There was no one about and again I felt scared, at the silence of being alone, at my own reflection in the mirror. When I went to close my locker, I found that it stuck. It was a rusty old thing with a bent distressed door, and at first I just thought it needed a kick, but after trying this a couple of times I looked more closely. Something was peeping out of the bottom of my locker, holding it open, poking out from just under a spare set of scrubs folded there. It was small and tubular, gray in color. I crouched down and pulled the snag from the door. In my palm lay a tiny, disconnected baby doll's hand. It wasn't the first time I'd been left such tokens. But this was stranger than usual because little lengths of Elastoplast had been wrapped painstakingly around all of the doll's fingers. I felt spooked. I put the hand in my pocket, resolving to show it to someone, maybe one of the theater managers. I'd been quiet about things like this for too long.

Afterwards it was hard to keep my focus. I was wor-ried about going to theater and I kept looking behind me. My mind wandered. A memory came to me from when I had spent a summer as a teenager with my family in apartheid South Africa. At the theater one evening, we had seen a famous actor called Pieter-Dirk Uys who was satirizing a far-right racist faction called the Wit Wolwe, the White Wolves, and his act was a short mime. He came onto the bare stage wearing a wolf's mask and in his arms he carried a black baby doll. Silently, he crept to the middle of the stage and stopped there. And then he lifted up the snout of his mask and clicked open a little hook at the back of the doll's head, so that the top of the plastic skull fell open on its hinge like when you open an egg to eat it with soldiers. Then he scooped stuff from the doll's head into his mouth and ravenously ate it. By turns looking up to meet the audience's eyes, making us complicit in this obscene feast, and down again to the doll's open cranium, he gobbled.

Still alone in the locker room, I went over to the basins. I looked myself in the eye, and said aloud, "Pull yourself together, Nancy." I was grateful to see myself in surgical scrubs and reminded myself that I had a job to do. I had plenty of practice girding myself in this setting, quarantining apprehension, and the rough words I spoke did me good. A short time later I left the locker room, partly becalmed, ready to start my cases.

In theater, everything was orderly. May had already anesthetized our first patient. Her legs were up in stirrups, a drape over her crotch to protect her modesty until I arrived. The ultrasound scanner was next to her, its screen giving out a grainy image of nothing yet. Joe, the anesthetic assistant, was in the corner finding a station on the radio, and Felisa was at the computer, embarking on the necessary admin. I rested my hand on May's shoulder as I bent over the anesthetic station to check the notes. The seventeen-year-old. Eight weeks pregnant. One previous termination. Rh-positive. No medical history. I checked the name band around the girl's wrist to make sure we had the right patient.

I worked through my first case without event. The second operation should have been the same. This woman was also surgically uncomplicated, with healthy anatomy and a pregnancy of only a few weeks' gestation. But although I performed all the same steps I had in the first operation, in more or less the same time, inside I was beginning to feel different, as I had during several of my recent OR days. Detached, not completely rooted.

I stared at my hands. The left one had the job of holding the vulsellum, of bringing the cervix forward, the more easily to access it. This hand looked familiar, like a part of my body belonging to me absolutely. But when I glanced over to my right hand in the size 7 glove which was just the tiniest fraction too big, I felt differently towards it. There was some slack in the web spaces and at the fingertips, and droplets of moisture were collecting on the other side of the yellow latex. All these features were normal. But the way that this hand was moving, the way it held the plastic cannula, guiding the tubing which traveled down to floor level and emptied into the measuring jar, the way the wrist rotated at the same time as the hand moved in and out, forwards and back, seemed ghastly to me. It was as if this active extremity had nothing to do with the rest of my body, with any aspect of my thinking or sentient self. It was as if it moved despite me.

I had experienced this unnerving feeling of dissociation for the first time at the very end of an OR day a few weeks previously. Initially, I had thought I was having some kind of neurological event, the onset of a migraine or something worse, a transient ischemic attack, even a stroke. I had managed to keep calm until the end of the case before going to the toilets and giving myself a mini neurological examination to make sure my sensory and motor function was still intact.

And the same thing had happened quite a few times since, particularly when I had a lot of cases to get through and didn't have the leisure to think about each of the patients separately. As I completed the second case of that day I resolved that, for my own frail sake, I would have to work harder for the rest of the morning, for the three operations that remained, to find stories for the women I was operating on whose real histories were unknown to me.

I have no memory of the next two patients. They have become insignificant to me now, by comparison with the fifth case of the morning, the catastrophe. Perhaps I had done so well in returning myself to a normal functioning state that I was lazy for that last woman.

But here's what I am sure of. This was the point at which I should have stopped operating. I was feeling unwell. I had encountered a sentinel moment of crisis, heralding what was to come. As a responsible health professional I should have recognized my inability to continue, sought out my attending, outlined the risks I posed to patient safety, and canceled the last case. I might even have been applauded for my probity, my adherence to the all-important tenets of patient safety and clinical governance.

As it was I don't think the idea crossed my mind. Doctors rarely consider their own feelings, never mind complaining about them. And the fact was that I wasn't going to let something like this make me stop operating, any more than I would have allowed a head cold to prevent me driving my car. So I decided to press on through the next case. I'd be finished soon enough.

So, I embark on my next operation with my eye on the horizon, as it were. I begin the procedure estimating that it will be over in ten minutes, that I can find a place afterwards to breathe in some air, or a remote hospital toilet to cry in. Only after doing my duty and sorting out my patient will I attend to myself.

I work. Minutes pass. Before long, I think I've reached the end of the operation. I see May tailing off her anesthetic gases. I'm leaning over to the trolley to pick up the Flagyl suppository and maxi pad. I pause because May is asking me a question.

"Can I get some advice from you about my sister-in-law? So, she's thirty-two weeks pregnant and she's had some bleeding."

The antibiotic bullet is in my right hand. I hold it in a pincer grip between my thumb and forefinger. I don't want to look at this hand, would rather not discover if it is still mutinous. I prefer to control it by feeling what it needs to do, by stereognosis alone. The sanitary pad is in my left, reliable hand. The hand that belongs to me. The hand I can depend on. I am lifting the pad through the air from the trolley to where I will tuck it snugly just under my patient's buttocks, while listening to May. It looks fat and clean. I am pleased by its whiteness against the faraway gloom of the operating theater behind it.

My retina is soaked in this whiteness. It is not ready for all the blood that awaits its next glance. My eyes cannot take in the redness to start with. It is as if what I am looking at is the character of red, not the color. Like looking at the sun, or staring into a fire. Automatically, I get some forceps and a four-by-four swab to blot the blood away, but as soon as I do this, more comes, like a stream now. I reach for more swabs, folding each one tightly in turn, and I grasp them in my forceps and push them further in, one after another, rotating my arm and wrist briskly as I do so, hoping for a bit of vasospasm, praying for contraction. But this has the opposite effect, as if my attempt to stem the blood has disturbed whatever small amount of clot formation was taking place.

"She's bleeding," I announce. I expect my voice to be loud, but it comes out as no more than a whisper.

I know I am in trouble. I must do something. I need to find a way to pull myself together. My mind races in pursuit of a trick, an exercise, a measure of any kind that might call me back to myself. I remember a neurosurgeon telling me to trust in a patient's inner physiological strength. And this is what I do now.

I think of how together my patient and I are strong enough to stop this blood loss. I think of her insides. When a person is bleeding profusely, certain organs get first dibs on the remaining circulation. The kidneys are high up in this pecking order and grab blood from less important places. I can't see my patient's kidneys, but they're not far below the surface, just under where your hands would be if you were a dancer or an ice-skater about to raise your partner to the sky in a beautiful lift. They are made of a smooth outer cortex, and an inner medulla, which is the complicated-looking textured part. Their main function is to regulate the body's fluid balance and to remove waste products from the blood for excretion in the urine.

For all this to work, over a liter of blood needs to be delivered to these organs every single minute. If someone's bleeding, and there's only so much to go round, the kidneys make sure they get their quota by dilating the vessels that supply them. It's as if they're a sponge sucking more fluid in.

This is all very well, but once my patient's mean arterial pressure drops too low, the clever autoregulation of the kidneys will break down. Then all those stress hormones circulating around the body will have the opposite effect, causing the previously dilated vessels in the kidneys to constrict, reducing even further the amount of blood that can reach them. If this was an operation that anyone had anticipated would go so badly, my patient would have had a urinary catheter in place, and the anesthesiologist would be noticing it run dry.

In front of me, blood is no longer just between the woman's legs, but snaking everywhere else now, completely ungoverned. It has made a river which runs across the drape until it meets the edge. Then it is on the floor and a new pool is forming there, and getting bigger too.

May is doing her arcane, professional dance, administering a milky-white substance into the woman's arm which I know is propofol, to prevent her from waking up to this. She has turned up the oxygen so that I can hear its loud, mechanical sigh. And now I see her collecting a tiny bit of the precious blood that remains in my patient, to send to the lab to be cross-matched for a transfusion. Joe stands by with a bag of fluid, though whether it is crystalloid or colloid it is not my place to know.

It's not my job to understand these things. All that is expected of me is to perform one simple task: to stop my patient from bleeding. Chapter one in my surgical textbook: "Exsanguinating patients need immediate definitive treatment by surgery." The duty of my anesthetic colleague is to buy me some time, to keep my patient alive while I do this cardinal thing.

The other really greedy organ is the heart. Normally, blood entering the right side of the heart gets laced with oxygen from the lungs before being pumped from the left side back round the body.

But my patient's bleeding so much there's not much left in her. The only way the body can compensate for this is to make the heart beat faster. That's why, if you feel the pulse of someone who's exsanguinating, it becomes fast, or tachycardic. The heart is working extra-vigorously to try and make up for the fact it has less in it to deliver around all those thirsty tissues. Eventually though the heart rate will drop very low and become bradycardic. It will give up its fight. This usually happens just before a patient dies.

I haven't moved much while thinking these thoughts. And there's no point in thinking of my patient's innards anymore to try and galvanize myself because the biggest organ of all, her skin, is right in front of me telling its own tale. This vast epidermis is redelivering its share of the body's blood to the parts deep inside which need it most. The tiny capillaries, which are usually plumped to prettiness, are squeezing tight, so that the complexion is losing its blush. Her legs are ashen, cerulean, and the pale skin under her toenails is turning blue.

I would like to help her, but there is no possibility of action in me. The connections between my motor cortex and spinal cord and limbs seems bust. My arms hang pointlessly from my shoulders. And there are my hands, dead at the ends of those arms. They look ruddy next to the mottling skin of my patient's thighs. Under my skin, I imagine the complicated layering and overlapping of my extensor muscles. If I stretch my fingers out just a little, there are the tendons too. And by turning my hands over, I can see the thenar and hypothenar eminences, the delicate curves of the intrinsic muscles of the hand, the bulges of the flexors, the pulps of each surgical finger, the adductors in each thumb.

I can even see beneath them to the bones of the hand—and I know the mnemonic. Scared New Lovers Try Positions That They Can't Handle. Scaphoid, navicular, lunate, triquetrum, pisiform, trapezium, trapezoid, capitate, hamate. The bones seem so bright to me in that moment that once I settle on them, I can no longer see the muscles and skin. I can only frame the bones, the scaffolding of these hands, the essential units, the part of my extremities that will remain after I am dead. It doesn't hurt me to focus on these bones now, dwelling on the acceptability of their deadness. Hands already inert, whose functional covering is not worth recognizing or even looking at in its failure to act.

The only movement in the room now is not of my making. May is at my shoulder now and is commanding me, "Nancy, for God's sake! Don't just sit there. I'm right up to the line here!" And Joe, a man known for bulk and slow feet, a guy who does nothing in a hurry, is not dawdling anymore but moving mightily and is hooking up more fluid; his body-built arms are in an arc waiting for the next instruction, the next thing he can do which will feel like help. Felisa is fleet in moving from where she was standing sentry to inert instruments: she is at the phone in the corner of the theater, making a call, telling one of my gynecology colleagues who she knows is operating next door to drop what he is doing. "Come now! Come now!" she says. And the rest of the room's motion is just the spreading of blood. While I sit absolutely still, quite frozen, watching my patient bleeding almost certainly to death in front of my very eyes.

When I recollect this scene I see it as if from the outside. And even though my memory gives the truth to me so that in one sense it has no mystery, it also looks absurd. The people in the room who have been trained to be still and calm are moving around frantically and showing their fear. They scan the room for a solution. Felisa, who has not managed to get my gynecology colleague to leave what he is doing to come and help, now calls the hospital switchboard and puts out an urgent pager call for Frederick, who she hopes is somewhere nearby and not on the other side of the hospital. And while they all bustle, the patient and I remain stock-still. She looks as if she ought to be dead by now, but the blood is still coming out of her briskly enough to suggest some cardiac output. And I, the one person in the room who has the capacity to save this situation from disaster, continue to do nothing. My shoulders are slumped and I am looking down at the useless hands in my lap.

How long this carries on I do not know. Many minutes. Perhaps half an hour. As long as it takes a person to die? This is what I am thinking at the moment when I feel the very walls shake. I wonder whether there is an earthquake, whether the building is falling down, whether what is happening in my operating theater is, in fact, part of a wider, larger natural disaster, some outside catastrophe. Both doors fly open, and Frederick crosses the room in two strides. With hands under my arms, he lifts me off the operating stool and passes me over, like the pointless cargo I am, to Joe. He sits down and holds out his wonderful large, veined hands for gloves, raising them up, palms open, fingers bent, as if in supplication. And once sheathed, these hands of his stay still for just a second or two, poised in the air before he picks up suction in one hand, forceps in the other. Before they descend into the pool of blood all around him, into the bleeding insides of my woman patient, just long enough to ask May one question.

"Is she still alive?"

I nearly miss my train stop. I get up from where I have been sitting intently for over an hour, knocking an empty paper cup off the table. Stooping to pick it up, I see my jacket underneath the seat, almost forgotten. I only just manage to get off the train before it pulls away. See the shambolic woman, I think, standing on the platform, whom the other passengers would look at with new eyes if they knew she was a doctor. Ha! See the harried abortionist under cover. See the visitor to the coast, off on a simple jaunt to hear her sister sing in a choir concert. I do not catch my usual ten-minute bus to the beach. I walk the pavements to the concert hall. Mark is looking after the kids so that I can hear Julia sing. I've never gone to one of my sister's concerts before. I'm due to stay with her afterwards, but just for one night this time, then back to London and headfirst into the week when I will find out what is to become of me.

I open the swing doors and enter the foyer of the music hall. They have the same heft as the doors to the Day Surgery Unit. Here, though, those humans who look at me don't do so with suspicion or barely shrouded distaste. The glances I get are from a couple my parents' age, and they seem affectionate. A couple of men, too, watch me. This is because they don't know who I am. Then my sister rushes towards me. She wears layers of black and long, dangly earrings. She squeezes me. Her scent falls on me lightly. She knows who I am and she still loves me. Is this all I have to hope for? I think of David, the mud on his boots, think of the way his trousers hang on his hips. I turn my attention back to the reassuring landscape of my sister's open face. She is talking to me, fondly, impatiently. She is so used to me only half listening to her, half being anywhere.

"You'll have to join in a couple of times, you know," she is saying.

I chance a reply, hoping it won't be too much of a non sequitur. "You mean like at the panto? He's behind you! Oh no, he isn't! Oh yes, he is!"

"You'll recognize the first one from school. 'All creatures that on earth do dwell.' You won't be able to resist singing it, Nance. The second one's harder. Let's see if you manage." She passes me a ticket, kisses my cheek, cuts a dash. I watch her disappear to join the other singers. She is not afraid to have her back to me, or to anyone. She has not felt eyes boring through that back. Lucky Mark. What a thing, to have a woman like that. A mother. Soprano in a choir. A normal, loving female.

I find my seat and look up into the vaulted proscenium of the concert hall. I am alone but, of course, much less so than normal because no one here knows who I am. I am by myself but no one shuns me. I could go away to a new place, I could start over, and no one would know anything about me. I could do smear tests and deliver babies and cover my hard core with layer upon layer of softness, and bury myself.

The choir files in. They form a block. They look ahead. They take their physical proximity to each other for granted, the air that pools among them. The conductor walks on stage and bows. He is not young, but he is lean. There is virility in the depth of his bow and he is very happy to be in front of us all. I join in the applause, enjoying the convention. I like the innocence of the clapping. The choir straighten themselves. They would probably like to clap too. He is theirs and they must be proud.

And then my thoughts switch to a different track, they are laid on runners of a particular kind when the music starts. Over a pulse of bass strings a violin starts a story which has anxiety in it, or suspense. My program says Benjamin Britten's *Saint Nicolas*. This is the tale of his adventures. But there is no point in my reading this, or knowing it. All the music can do is tell me my own story. It has already started to do this with the tension of the first few bars.

The choir joins the orchestra. I am looking into a hundred open faces. I am looking into my sister's own mouth. I feel a shock of embarrassment at this display of physicality, this extreme, loud show of the human body whose sounds usually come to me in private, over-laid with shame. Are they not shy, standing next to each other and letting themselves out like that? Do they not feel uneasy letting us all see them, as we tighten back against their talent, silent in the face of their song.

I look up into the acoustic recesses of the hall. I let the music in. The tenor may sing of Saint Nicolas but he is telling me about everything that has happened to me and everything I have done. I think of my patient. The tenor's tune sings my story round and about me. He sings to me of my mistake, of my patient's near-death, my own collapse. Her stay in the Intensive Care Unit. My mon-umental error. Girls sing from the balcony. I refer to my program and see they represent the wind in the gale. I look at Julia, who is directly in front of me. She bisects all the important angles in the room. I feel my huge love for her in chords which gather in layers. And I envy her this place where she can put all her feelings; that she can look pretty in black and mimic a storm with her voice, and rejoice in its resolution with her next phrase. And I have no idea how I have got it all so very wrong.

When the choir pauses, it is as if they have heard my thoughts. When the conductor turns, smiling, en-couraging, lifting his baton to the audience, I feel he is addressing me, directing himself at me. And when the whole congregation of the audience stands and the huge hall is filled with the sudden massive vibrating hum of every single person singing, of a sound that has multi-plied massively in volume in just a few moments, I find I am one of the people that is making this happen. I do not rise slowly. I am already standing. I do not need to look at my program for the words of the hymn I sang for years as a child. My strand of song rises up from my diaphragm like a great wave. Even though my throat is tight from my silent doctoring, I sing out nonetheless, and because I cannot hear my own strained voice in the multitude, I sing louder still and wish there were more verses than there are. And I know that there is nothing like this in medicine. Nothing at all like this in all the hospitals I have been trained in, even though we walk with death as our companion and though we are deep in disease and are present for the beginning of life and its end. When we all sit down, my eyes are full of tears.

I do not find the chance to speak to my sister. I can't pick the right moment. Before long, it is time to go back to London. No one begrudges me my last half-hour alone on the beach. It's low tide when I sit on one of the groins, the late afternoon sunshine at my shoulder, my boots immersed in the one sand pool that forms faithfully twice a day at the base of the last post. My back is warm from the sun, my thoughts still liquid warm from yesterday's concert. But I have not carried into the new day any false sense that what I experienced then foretells my future tomorrow. I must go back to London and meet my fate, and I have no idea what decision awaits me there.

The sky is windless. The tide is low and flat. There is no noise from the waves. What I do hear is the distant sound of the people on the beach, stretching out for miles on this fine afternoon. No one is near enough for their noise to reach me. I look at my boots and, moving them, observe the sound this makes. I imagine an audiogram, how I might plot the sound on a graph, frequency in hertz against volume in decibels. See how I order every detail of my experience into the file named Doctor. How on earth will I manage if I am erased, removed, struck off the medical register? I will lose my entire frame of reference. And what would I have to replace it? What is a doctor, if not a doctor? Take that title away and there may be very little left over.

But, for now, I allow myself to bend my feet this way and that. Look at the water trickling through the creases of my rubber boots; concentrate on that pleasing low-frequency trickle, burble, mini-splash. Stay with this, concentrate on only this until, slantingly, I can push through consciousness into the place that lies just behind it. I have been afraid to let my mind go like this for months because of the images and all the thoughts waiting there to vex me, but I realize I can do it safely again now.

If I keep my feet still, there is the thick varnish of the sea's surface, one searing spot under the sun, the rest a mirror on which I can see the faraway clouds, the odd speeding gull measuring out angles on the protractor of the sky. I move my feet and the infinity of clouds and sky breaks, replaced by close gray folds of sand, small details of green weed and underside of miniature dead crab, segmented and blue. The near and the far, the yes and the no. Striking off or not. Forgiveness or not. Acquittal or not. Absolution or not. And even if they excuse me, this panel, can I excuse myself? What conclusion should I draw from the verdict I am given?

I sit in the waiting room for the last time. The fact that I was at my sister's house yesterday is irrelevant. As far as my judges are concerned, this is all I am: the fearful doctor, waiting to find out about her future career. But I am unlearning the skill of years. What has the last month brought me if not this, the realization that a life is not like the way a doctor describes the life of their patient? Presenting complaint, history of presenting complaint, systems history, drugs and social history, all in order before the examination findings are reported. All in order before conclusions are drawn from all of these things. I could laugh now to think of how I have prided myself on my social-history-taking, the bit so many doctors leave out altogether. How good I have felt because I always had some detail to tell about my patient's domestic circumstances, if I did happen to get asked about them. I might have a hobby up my sleeve, a revelatory occupational hazard, a touching detail, the name of a pet, the shadow of a recent bereavement.

Never mind that I have not done this as well as I thought I had. What a fool I have been to think I have been leading a life of my own just because I have held the fat bouquet of all these other lives in my arms, all the blooms just where they should be, at the end of the stems I have tidied and aligned and bound fast. And now I find this is no way to tell the truth at all, if one is trying to tell one's own truth. So I will let a thing not follow the way it should. I will go from one place to another, without explanation. I will let myself, at long last, unravel a little.

The chair I have chosen to sit on is green. I look at my watch. I am bang on time for my panel appointment. I feel the adrenaline in my blood, gathering full momentum again, heating my limbs, bringing a thin perspiration to cool my back, leaving no room for thought but only for an intense awareness.

Nurses chatter in a nearby corridor. A radio, playing in the distance, leans towards the world outside. I notice the tight green stitching on my seat. Hear footsteps in the main hospital, beyond the walls of the waiting room, approach and fade. A fat black fly, on top of a lampshade, rubs dust from its feet. Sounds and minute irrelevant events orbit me, and stretch out from me in my stillness, seeming to occupy an age in space and time. I am in a pram in a park looking up into the rush of trees. I have fainted in a church. I am down in a dark cellar. My grandfather is dead, says my mother. I am standing in front of a classroom of children, reciting a speech. I am waiting to turn over an exam paper and muttering a poem to calm myself: "'O why do you walk through the fields in gloves, missing so much and so much? O fat white woman whom nobody loves...'"

The door opens. It is Dr. Garber. "Come in, Nancy," he says—and I am reeled back into the world with one spool, drawn back into my body again, where I find my limbs trembling, yet my voice despite everything knows how to say "Hello," and my face is able to regain tone in order to flex into a little smile before returning to the neutral. I walk into the room and take my seat.

I look at them in turn. And everything is just itself again while also being quite different, seeming to hold within itself the possibility of anything at all, the potential for absolute change lying just beneath the surface of what I see, of what I am managing to inhabit as normally as I can. The features of the room flatten to the occasion. I shut the other versions out, forcing the details to take a back seat, allowing myself to focus on what I am now ready to hear. It is Dr. Mansfield who speaks.

"Good morning, everyone. We are here for the last time today to make a decision on a case of clinical negligence brought to our attention just over a month ago. The three of us were appointed to this task by the Chief Executive of this hospital trust, under the aegis and approval of the General Medical Council. First of all, I would like to thank everyone here for the responsible way in which these sessions have been conducted. It is certainly a source of satisfaction to me that we have not needed to refer this case back to the GMC, that we have managed to deal with it here, locally, up until this point."

Because she is sitting next to her co-panelists, Dr. Mansfield isn't able to get much recognition from either of her colleagues for this opening speech, but I smile at her. She looks so much more comfortable like this, speaking formally, than she has, unscripted, during previous sessions. She's back on home ground, I suppose, inhabiting the muscular clauses all those bone-breaking orthopods she works with would enjoy. I have missed a bit now, I realize.

"...Dr. Garber. After he has finished taking us through the findings from the psychiatric assessment, I will deliver our verdict on what happened in Theater 3 exactly five weeks ago today. There will be plenty of time at the end for discussion or to explain anything that is not completely clear. Nancy, do you have any questions at this stage?"

"No, thank you," I reply. I am keen now to hear what everyone has thought of me. It has been impossible, this past month, to establish what I think of myself. I wonder if I have said the last thing I am ever going to say in this room. There won't be any point in questioning their judgment, will there, once it has been made? And I've had my chance to speak already. Suddenly I feel a great heaviness in my heart at all the things left unsaid during these hours.

Dr. Mansfield finishes her speech, and now it is Dr. Garber's turn. He glances from side to side at his colleagues, even though they are both looking down. He looks up from his papers to meet my gaze.

"Dr. Gilchrist has written a pretty comprehensive report," he says, indicating with a slim thumb that there are many pages before him. His face is pink. This is a big day for all of us, I suppose.

"...beginning with his Mental State Examination, in which he describes Nancy's mood as having been congruent throughout, with normal variation in affect during the different parts of the interview, although some reduction in facial expression. No evidence whatsoever of psychotic features...da, da, da. Nothing relevant in the past history, normal childhood and school history, no past psychiatric history. No drug or alcohol issues. Oh yes. Moving on, this is an interesting bit here. Dr. Gilchrist says that there are strong correlations between Nancy's case and others he has seen before. Actually, this is his special area, post-traumatic stress disorder."

He holds his hand up, asking for us to bear with him. He reads for a few moments to himself, muttering and humming the words in front of him as he takes them in, ruminates on them, gets them ready to bring out again. After a few moments he looks up, first to Dr. Mansfield, then to me.

"So, there is, apparently, a subset of post-traumatic stress disorder called perpetration-induced traumatic stress. The original research came from studying veterans from the Vietnam War. And these guys, the soldiers, well many of them came back in a mess after that time. We all know that, right? But what this research shows is that the stress reaction, the psychological disintegration, was observed to be extreme in those who had actually killed people in Vietnam. And now, Dr. Gilchrist says, that original research has been applied to all sorts of workers whose occupation involves them in killing: vets euthanizing animals, executioners. Even abortion providers..."

"Tim, where is this all leading?" asks Dr. Mansfield.

"Look, this is not the main conclusion that Dr. Gilchrist is drawing, but it's really important, I think. Actually, we have a PTSD group at the surgery that we're really making some progress with, so...my point, Dr. Gilchrist's point, is that many of the symptoms Nancy has experienced, what he calls the eidetic dreams—the dreams which seem to replay the event—the sense of social isolation, the freezing-up in theater, are cardinal features of this syndrome. Given that this session is taking us towards a verdict, I think it's important that we spell out for Nancy that what has happened to her may, in the view of this psychiatrist, have arisen directly out of the kind of work she has chosen to do."

Well, that's a pretty package, I think to myself. A nice neutral report. Nothing wrong with me, honest, Guv, it's just the job I do. I wonder what will come next.

"Dr. Gilchrist's conclusion is—well, look, I'll read you a bit. 'I could find no evidence of a continuing or chronic condition. If pressed, I would categorize this according to ICD-10 criteria as F43.0, an acute stress reaction. However, I have also noted similarities between this case and a subsection of post-traumatic stress disorder known as perpetration-induced traumatic stress, whose features include obsessional thinking, depression and fatigue, identity conflicts and withdrawal from colleagues. While I do not see any immediate danger of a repeat crisis as long as this young doctor reconsiders her line of work, I do recommend that—' "

"Tim, let's hold the recommendations for now. I think it would be best to give these, Dr. Gilchrist's and ours, such as they are, a bit later, after we have given Nancy our decision. Do you agree?"

Dr. Garber shuffles his papers together at this request. He looks pleased and important, happy for Dr. Mansfield to take over again. After focusing on the GP, I notice again how upright Dr. Mansfield is, how perfectly done.

"Nancy, it's been an interesting few weeks. It's clear from the long discussion Tim and Vivien and I have had, that we had yesterday, about you and what's happened, that there isn't one of us on this side of the table that hasn't benefited from the experience. Speaking personally, some of the things you have said over the weeks about the fragmentation of patient care have struck a real chord. When I was an intern, we worked in firms. We had a resident and a fellow and a specialist whom we stayed with for months. We saw our patients come into hospital, and we were the ones to wave them on their way. Whatever else we've gained, we've lost this. You've reminded me of it, Nancy, and I think we've all had sympathy with what you've argued so strongly in this room, that the doctor's relationship with their patient is sacred and should be protected.

"I want you to know that Dr. Garber and I sit on the Clinical Governance Committee of this hospital trust and we will make it our duty not to let this matter drop. We are going to take what you have reminded us of, Nancy, to that committee, and see what we can do.

"The next thing to say is that Dr. Gilchrist's report is not the only one we have had the benefit of, Nancy. We have gathered references from all the specialists you have worked with, and from the Dean of the medical school here, as to your conduct as an undergraduate. There has been nothing whatever in any of these references to suggest anything other than a hardworking, honest doctor, with great potential." She pauses and looks at me and adds, "The kind of doctor I would welcome as a trainee, I might add."

"But," Dr. Garber turns to her, "don't forget what we were talking about as well. About the suitability of—"

"Don't worry, Tim. I'm coming to that. You'll have your say. I'm just making sure it's clear that I...that we recognize there are particular pressures in a surgical job. Challenges which Nancy here has obviously coped with admirably with the exception of this one occasion."

"Oh, I see. Here we go. Time for a little GP-bashing, is it?" Dr. Garber places his hands palms-down on the table. "No. You know what. I'm going to say my piece now, as we agreed I would. Nothing much. I don't have a whole spiel. I just want Nancy to hear that I think it is possible to agree with abortion in principle and yet not find it possible to be involved oneself. I know this. I mentioned... in one of our sessions, I said that I have referred women for abortions. I used to, that is. But I don't do it anymore. And not because...I don't judge these patients, you understand. It is not my position to. But what I have found is that, since my own circumstances have changed, since I became a father, I have not been able to make these abortion referrals."

"But, Tim, for the here and now, what is the...?"

"My point is...," he replies, putting the tips of all his fingers together carefully. Here's a church and here's a steeple, open it up and there are the people. "That it is possible that some of the duties of being a doctor may be just too much for us. Or we may be up to the task one day, but not the next. So, all I'm saying is, it's clear that Nancy felt she was doing the right thing. Maybe we all see that she had the right intentions. But perhaps it takes a certain kind of person to do her job, whether we like it or not, and it may be that she is just not that kind of person. I want her to think about it, Miriam, that's all."

Dr. Mansfield looks at me as if she is expecting, even inviting me to join in, to contribute, to take somebody's part. But there isn't anything for me to say, nothing to add that will make a difference to the verdict they have already determined. For once, I am simply curious. Interested to see how they have wrapped my experience up in a bundle and put a bow on it, how each of them has found a version of the truth that might give coherence to this pathology, to what I have done and what has happened to me. This is exactly what Dr. Mansfield is doing as I start to listen to them again.

"...would have been so easy for her to conscientiously object to learning this aspect of gynecological care. Just think of it. I mean, imagine if a whole group of my trainees said, you know, we have a religious objection to doing any operations that might result in the need for a blood transfusion. It would not be called 'conscientious refusal of care' which, Nancy, is what everyone has renamed conscientious objection now, it would be called completely unacceptable doctoring, for God's sake. I mean, who are these doctors to say they will do this part of the job but not that? Leaving the others to do all of it, to feel isolated because of it, to end up in a mess as Nancy has done. The department has something to answer for, in my opinion, and so does the Royal College!"

There is a pause in which Dr. Garber and Dr. Mansfield shuffle their papers, realign themselves, find a way to sit next to each other peaceably. Only Vivien, sphinxlike, remains composed. Light from the window behind the panel table frames the three of them, arranged in a stiff, official row. I look at the soft hair on Tim Garber's head. I have merely been unsuited to my work. That's what he thinks. It exempts him from having to ponder the philosophical nature of the work itself, doesn't it, or the question of what it might mean if a person did feel comfortable in such a job. He only has to consider this case, this example of a supposedly oversensitive doctor, unequal to a difficult task.

And proud Dr. Mansfield, the cat who walks by herself, is just championing the cause of all lonely cats, is she not? It is as if she has expurgated the whole abortion issue from her tale. For her, perhaps, this whole situation boils down to the simple question of whether a doctor has balls or not, whether or not enough support has been forthcoming from above. And though she may have started out thinking of me as weak, this is probably not her final opinion. I imagine she sees her own bravery in my decision to do not just a part but all of the job I have been given.

So, while I still await my verdict with anticipation, with a respect for the fact that what is said in this room will determine my future as a gynecologist, as a doctor, while I see Vivien straightening herself up in her seat, bringing a great sense of excitement and dread into me, while my adrenal glands do what they do, releasing catecholamines into my body, telling me the time has come, the moment has arrived, I also know that whatever has been determined will not be enough to condemn or acquit me in my own eyes. There has been too much left undiscussed. My own account has been parlous.

But the time has come and I am very still. Everything is in slow motion now. I see Vivien's profile, her high brow and straight nose. I see Dr. Mansfield and Dr. Garber nod to her. I see her young hands frame a single sheet of paper. I see her turn towards me, oh so calmly, her violet eyes directed at me. And the surprise of her deep, steady voice, heard for the first time, comes to me with the shock of her words.

"We, the members of this panel, approve Dr. Nancy Mullion's fitness to practice. We are satisfied that—with the application of temporary conditions and restrictions—Dr. Mullion is safe to continue in her work as a gynecologist at this hospital. We do not feel this case merits referral back to the GMC. It is our unanimous decision that Dr. Nancy Mullion be free to decide whether or not she continues in her current line of work. Our decision has been ratified by the Chief Executive of this hospital trust."

I take the news deep into myself. It is like a parcel that is not yet unwrapped. I cannot unwrap it. I remember as a child holding a present unopened in the palms of my hands. It upset my aunt that I did this. She called me ungrateful. I am on my feet because Dr. Mansfield and Dr. Garber are advancing towards me. They are smiling and I cannot just sit here and let them approach while I sit like a stone. Dr. Mansfield has a sheet of paper, which she gives to me. These are the conditions and the restrictions and a copy of the verdict, she says. I should take my time thinking of what I want to do; until the end of the week should be enough. And if I want to reconsider a career in surgery, I should come and see her. Her door is open to me. Her skin is soft and powdered, the wrinkles in it fine. She is tiny, suddenly, standing up. Dr. Garber too takes my hand in two of his and offers me congratulations. Vivien stays sitting.

I thank them all. I don't know quite when to turn and leave the room. I feel the hospital paper beginning to curl between my thumb and index finger from the sweat in my hands. I walk through the door. I straighten my neck and hold my head high. This is my hospital again, if that's what I want it to be. I wait for the feeling of jubilation that is surely due. But it doesn't come. My feet take me past the morgue and all the way to the end of the corridor. There is a small courtyard at the back of the building, near Administration and Plant Operations, and I head towards it. There won't be anyone I know there. As I pass through the clinical departments of the hospital to its nether regions, where they keep dead bodies, where forklift trucks are parked in dusty subterranean corridors, where towers of supplies, pads and mattresses and tubing rest naked, not yet important in the job they are to be used for, I see the personnel change too. Fewer and fewer white coats people these corridors. I notice no nurses here. No blue uniforms for the proud dietician, the doctor-hungry physical therapist, the pretty speech pathologist. Men with big stomachs, and stooped men, and men with folded cheeks and rheumy eyes clank beds and machinery. A young lad swears as he bends to pick up a stack of hand towels which he has piled too high against a wall. A Filipino man stops his partial mopping to let me pass. I meet his eye by way of thanks.

I go out of one of the outsize metal doors. The smoking area is empty. I rest my feet among the butts and look at the page in front of me. Headed notepaper with a list of my judges' names at the top. Underneath, there is an exact copy of the words Vivien spoke, letting me off the hook. Beneath this are two paragraphs. The first one bears the heading Restrictions. I read, "For six months, Dr. Mullion should not do any emergency surgery during on-call hours. She should only perform elective surgery under specialist supervision. For review by the Occupational Health Department in six months."

The final paragraph on the page is entitled Conditions and reads "Dr. Mullion may continue to practice as long as she follows the restrictions and recommendations as given here. Dr. Gilchrist advises a course of cognitive behavioral therapy, to be arranged by the Occupational Health Department. He does not see the need for psychodynamic therapy. All panel members agree that a mentor be nominated within the Obstetrics and Gynecology Department with whom Dr. Mullion be free to air any concerns on a weekly basis. This specialist has not yet been found."

I fold the paper in half, then into quarters. I look at the litter at my feet and up at the unwashed back façade of the hospital in which I have been trained and in which I have fallen. I feel utterly deflated. I think about the oddity of how, at no point in this process, have I talked about how it actually feels to do an abortion. It seems a big gap suddenly, a hell of an omission. Perhaps this is why I feel so little sense of triumph. And if I have not been able to say these things to a panel, over four weeks of questioning, have been mute even with my own sister, then to whom am I meant to speak? Is there anyone in the world I might recount my experience to, any setting on earth in which these facts might, finally, be let out? Might there be a metaphorical way of gesturing at the essentials of my work? Could I perhaps paint a picture just in colors? Imagine the blue of a day before it starts. That has been the sad hue of my work.

I get up and go back into the hospital. Could I have told those doctors one kind of story that would have suggested another? Might I have described the time when my dad ran over a fox? He stopped the car and found the fox half dead and twitching. And cried by himself as he searched with numb hands for a heavy stone to finish the job. And how he still dreams about this fox that he killed, its eyes like foil in the night.

I leave the unseemly part of the hospital behind and re-enter the clinical zone, the part fit for public viewing. Or could I go a tiny bit further and describe to someone just one detail? Imagine the posture of a fetus when it is no longer warmly forming but out in the breathless air of our adult world. There was a man once, a young man whom I certified dead when I was an intern. He lived a life of only about twenty years. He had been born with cerebral palsy, and at a time and in a place where he was not given any physiotherapy. And so, as an adult, his body was contorted with strictures and contractures. He had what used to be described in the medical literature as a windswept appearance, like trees in stormy places whose branches stay hectic and extreme even on still days, unable to relax from all the gales they have wintered. He died in this position. And, like those trees, even in death he held his pose of absolute suffering, frozen in this mold of terrible life. Could I say that I am reminded of this man when I see my work before me? Can I say that no one expects becoming a doctor to be easy, but that I did not expect it to be this hard?

I pick up pace now. I walk down one corridor, turn into another, head for the Gynecology Department, my academic home. I am right on time for the lunchtime meeting. I am searching for a way to speak. How many years has it taken me to get to this point? There are things I must say head-on. But it is a problem. We don't see Oedipus put out his eyes. He comes back on stage and they are gone and there is blood on his face. We wouldn't want to actually see him put out his eyes, would we?

At the door of the seminar room I stop. I see them all in there, going through the weekly accumulation of morbidity and mortality. And I think to myself that there are a hundred ways for me to say anything but what is on my mind. Look at how many times I have tried even in the past four weeks. How I have hedged and skirted around the truth of what I have seen and what I have done. Look at how many versions a doctor can manufacture and still miss right out on the truth: the truth of how we can grow and fall apart, of how a person can be dismantled.

Looking through the panes of glass in the window I see Frederick. He smiles at me and raises his eyebrows. I give him a thumbs-up. He beckons me in. Is this my chance to speak out? It seems as if the great gap between what I have been asked and what I have given of my own accord should not be allowed. I should not allow it. Suddenly it strikes me that this is a crisis of silence. My own small crisis. The huge abortion crisis. And every crisis in between. Each story of each unwanted pregnancy which itself came from someone not saying what had to be said or not being listened to. Don't touch me. I don't want more children. I am not happy with this. I want you but I'm not on the pill because I'm not a slut, you know. Can we use a condom? I wish you would love me. Will doing this make you want to stay? And no one is talking about what happens later, either. Not the women patients, not the doctors, not the brothers and husbands and fathers, not the sisters and mothers and friends. This is what happened in my abortion. Here is the abortion story of the person I love. This is the abortion that I did yesterday. This is what it means to me, and this, and this and this.

I stand at the door but I don't go in. I am not ready. But I know that if I don't find a way to say these things, I will never go back into the seminar room again. I have been quiet for much too long.

Would it be better to express myself in writing, to put my thoughts on paper? Might the printed word be the way to get my story across? It would be a way to give my panel of judges, these colleagues, at least the option of knowing the truth. I could make some sort of symbolic gesture. I could change the font, use italics perhaps. And it would be a way of saying *do not read these next words if you don't want to understand my reality. Bow out now if you feel faint-hearted. It would be my sign, my way of warning them that they were on dangerous ground. That I was about to start saying all the things that remain so hidden. And my gesture would bear testimony to the self-censorship that even the abortion providers cannot rid themselves of. My very script would bear the stigma of stigma. If you want to expurgate what you read or limit what you see, just scan ahead a few pages and carry on from there. This is what I might say.*

And then, having given this warning, perhaps I might at last go freely? Might I start trying to express the particularities of my experience, to say what I need to, to put myself back together, because I have been broken by my own silence. Might I now bring forth, from the darkness of my mind, the things that I have seen and done and felt?

I have done early abortions. And I have not found it all that difficult. It is clearly much harder to have it done than it is to do it. People talk about women having abortions for social reasons. But there is nothing casual about it. Any provider can tell you this. If the patient is under local anesthesia, it's perfectly clear to you that there is nothing easy about the tears that sneak out horizontally from a woman's eyes, the tears that course not down her cheeks, but towards the ears, because she is lying down. There is nothing cavalier about the way a girl's thighs tremble. Nothing slapdash about the chattering of her teeth, or of the sound of a nice lady muttering, "Oh fuck, oh fuck" under her breath. Or about the pain that even the local anesthetic won't take away. Or the vomiting.

But an early termination is technically straightforward, once you've done your first one. Once you've crossed the line from being someone who has never done an abortion, to someone who has. The cervix doesn't need much dilating. The contents of the womb are light. You can offer tablets to a woman with a very early unwanted pregnancy, or use a small manual vacuum aspirator, made in light and pretty white plastic as if it were trying to fit in with other women's domestic paraphernalia. Or you can opt for an electrical suction technique. The only challenge is to ensure the job is complete.

The task doesn't end with the surgery, though. When you finish doing the abortion, you take the products of conception into another room called the sluice. This is the room in which you have to make sure that things are as they should be. It is a job the doctor should do. A person should be responsible for their own dirty work, not give it to another member of staff to do for them. If you are going to do this job, you should have to face the whole thing, I think. You should be the one to talk to the patient, if you are going to terminate her pregnancy. You should be the one to do the check on that pregnancy after it has been removed.

For this job, you need a fine-meshed sieve. It's not a medical instrument, it's a sieve, like the ones we all have in our kitchens. You put the contents of your clinical bowl or jar into that sieve and gently run a tap over it, to filter out the important bits. With a gloved hand and a gentle touch, you look for the gestational sac. At five or six weeks' gestation, this is the size of a woman's little fingernail. The sac and the decidua look quite similar at this stage. The way to tell them apart is to transilluminate the tissue. This involves floating it in a tiny glass dish over a light. By doing this, you will recognize the gestational sac because it looks like a tiny piece of coral. It is fronded. It is not upsetting to look at. It is pretty, and looks like a plant. There is nothing humanoid about it. This is reassuring. Perhaps this should make no difference, but it does.

I have done midterm abortions. And I can tell you that by the end of the first trimester, things are harder. I don't care what the philosophers say. Maybe life is life, and it's all the same whether a conceptus is one day or six months old, but it feels different. My experience tells me another truth. It is still possible to perform at least most of the abortion using a suction cannula attached to an electrical pump. But even before you switch that pump on, it is a hard situation to be in. We use ultrasounds all the time now. And before you even start, the ultrasound shows you a human image on its screen. After a while of course, this image and the subsequent disintegration of this image does not affect you as profoundly as it may do on the first occasion. Everything gets easier with time. This is not a mark of the abortion provider's moral decrepitude, surely? It is a fact of life, that some things get easier and easier.

But still. There is that image. The image of the human form, whatever you choose to call it, is a few feet away from you. The cannula with its flexible tubing is in your hand. There is a softness in the very equipment. The image is grainy. It is an indistinct business. Still, it might seem like just the right time to look away from the ultrasound screen. It may be an opportune moment to miss out on what once appeared to me, on that screen, like the simulacrum of a human being falling to its knees as its life ended, what always shows as a black-and-white image changing and reducing and disappearing from the screen, the proportion of lucency reducing, the presence absenting itself, the overall white darkening to black.

Sometimes, unavoidably, the tubing will not be enough. Its caliber or bore may be too narrow. You know this has happened when the normal loud suction noise quietens down because something is blocking the end of the tube. It may be necessary to clear this tube, to pull a piece of tissue from its end. I won't lie and fudge. There is a feeling of shame in this blockage and sorting it out. There is shame in the mechanics of this. I have my italicized freedom. What obstructs the tube may be soft tissue but it is more likely to be an arm or a leg or a piece of spine. The protesters against abortion who stand at their pickets like to show you these parts. They favor the tiny hand for its poignancy. They wave this dead hand at you from their banners. They make it greet you with their own rude accusations. But these images do not belong to them. These images are mine too. The sights I describe are mine even more than theirs because they are part of my reality. And I agree with those angry abortion-haters, that group we call the antis, in this respect alone: that the things I see, and which they flaunt so mischievously, are the saddest sights I have known.

Can I not be allowed to tell this truth, so that it is not only in the wrong hands?

The skull of the fetus is called the calvarium. From the end of the first trimester onwards it can be hard to remove the calvarium. It may require forceps. Even then, it can be difficult to negotiate it out through the cervix. Because it is round, it slips away from one's grip. And succeeding in this matter does feel like violence. At medical school, I cut a dead man's leg off in an anatomy room so that my dissection group could learn the anatomy of the rectum. That felt like violence too. The lab technician said, Come on now. It's okay. How else are you going to learn? This is like that. Holding heavy forceps, feeling the mixture of give and resistance in the tissue they grasp, with only the instrument between my hands and the dismembering of a fetus: the dismalness of doing this for the first time is dreadful. It also feels like a moral act. You cannot just walk away from a problem. You cannot be a gynecologist and leave this work to someone else. That is the cowardice. That is what I think.

I have not done late abortions. I have not yet done late abortions. I have seen them, though. I have been with Frederick when he does them because I have wanted to see if I am ready to do them myself. I feel bad about this. I know that it doesn't make sense, logically, to separate one kind of life from another. The fact is that it just gets harder to manage as a pregnancy continues.

These are some of the facts of what I have done. And, as to the feelings, what can I say? I feel sad. I should feel sad, and I do. But as long as there is gentleness and understanding, it is okay. I don't like parts getting caught in the tube. I don't like having to grapple with them. But

I don't mind checking, at the end, that they are all there.
This is my clinical duty, if I am to avoid the risk of my
patient getting an infection, but it is another sort of duty
too. I check there is a calvarium, spine, two upper and
two lower limbs. Some of my colleagues do not like to
assemble them as they would have been in life. I feel the
opposite. I feel I want to do this. And I want to pause,
and give some kind of reverence to what was, and is no
more, a potential life.

This is what I would tell anyone prepared to listen.
I would give them this inkling of the truth. They could
read it in this form, so they could stop at any time. And
if they did not want to read this, they could just return
to where the italics disappeared, to where the prose returned to being safe and upright and not nasty. And the
story would work whether or not the italicized section
had been read.

I step back from the door. Suddenly I realize where it
is that I need to go. Hitting the main hospital corridor,
I follow the signs to the ICU and the Step-Down Unit. I
pick up my pace. I don't think about where my identity
card is because I am allowed to be here again. This is my
hospital as much as anybody's. I walk like a doctor with
a destination, with none of the shaky tread of my last
few visits.

At the junction of the three main corridors, I glance
at the bank of chairs where I sat so recently early one
morning. A young Asian woman in a uniform wipes the
plastic seats with a dirty cloth. She looks at me and
we smile at each other. I turn left and see the ICU and
the Step-Down Unit at the end of the corridor, straight
ahead.

Two people, a man and a woman, stand with their backs to me as I approach my destination, down the long wide corridor. The man is young and holds flowers. The woman has gray hair and clasps his arm. She is slim and elegant. She wears a pink sleeveless anorak. As I advance towards them, I hear the crackle of the Step-Down Unit intercom and the young man, leaning towards the microphone but keeping his arm where it is, for his companion's affectionate grip, says, "We're here to see Emily Smith" in a clear, hopeful voice.

I reach them and stop. The man and woman turn to face me. I hear the click of the door being unlocked from within. My patient's husband and mother walk together into the Step-Down Unit. I too continue on my way, treading the few remaining paces to the door between the Step-Down Unit and the ICU, where I stop and knock. I hear what I need to and open the door. I am glad to find that David is alone.

ACKNOWLEDGMENTS

I cannot thank Lara Agnew enough for the hours and hours she has given to this book. I am also very grateful to Lisa Harris, John Parsons, Andrew Amoah, Nick Thomas, Kate Guthrie, Tracey Thomas, Dan Franklin, Claire Conrad, Ander Cohen, Laura Hassan, Neil Ashman, Sam Guglani, John Weston, Sally Weston, and Helen Akal.

ABOUT THE AUTHOR

Gabriel Weston is an ear, nose, and throat surgical specialist. Her memoir, *Direct Red: A Surgeon's View of Her Life-or-Death Profession,* was chosen as a best book of the year in 2009 by *The Economist* and *The Telegraph,* long-listed for the Guardian First Book Award, and received the PEN/Ackerley Prize for Autobiography. She lives in London with her physician husband and their children.